AS GOOD AS DEAD

AS GOOD AS DEAD

THOMAS DEWEY

#2 in the Singer Batts series

WILDSIDE PRESS

Everybody loved Chick Lorimer—
Nobody knows where she's gone.

—Carl Sandburg

CHAPTER ONE

Linda Graves came home one spring day and moved into the big house near Thompson's Mill, where her father had died more than fifteen years before.

It had been a lot more than fifteen years since Linda had been in town. It had been at least twenty—some people said longer. Linda would be about forty-eight now—maybe fifty.

Funny thing about it was that nobody actually saw her. People would meet and one would say, "Linda Graves' come back. Moved into the hill place." The other would say, "Ain't seen her," and somebody else, "Nobody's seen her. But she's back."

Linda Graves was back, and the fact that she was back was known. But nobody in town could really say he'd seen her.

There had never been anything mysterious about the family until Linda's disappearance twenty years before. Old man Seth Graves had been the friendliest guy you'd want, and mixed around a lot in the town's affairs. And Linda as a girl had been seen often by everybody.

They said everybody had loved Linda. She was a gay gal, spirited, as they say, like a filly—not one to take any lip from anybody. Everybody loved her.

I picked this up by hearsay. I've only been around for five or six years myself. I never knew Linda Graves, or her father or anything about them—only what I picked up from hearing people talk. It didn't really mean a lot to me that she'd come back to town, until one day in June...

* * * *

It had been a pretty good month for the Hotel Preston. We'd been full every night for three months and the dining room had done a good business all that time. We'd made a little money and I felt good. This didn't mean anything to Singer Batts, the owner, who didn't care about the money and only wanted a comfortable place to live and be left alone so he could read his ancient books in peace.

But it meant a lot to me, the manager, because Singer Batts had done a lot for me and the only way I could repay him was by taking care of his interests. The fact he didn't care about his own interests didn't have anything to do with it.

As I say, I felt pretty good, and this afternoon I was relaxing with a long, cool drink in our sitting room, just sitting, thinking what a good three months we'd had and drinking the drink, feeling the cold glass against my hand, when all of a sudden the door of our suite opened and Harry Baird, the day clerk, came in.

I knew something was wrong because people are not supposed to come barging into the suite without knocking and Harry wouldn't do it except in an emergency.

He was boiling. He stamped in, closed the door, slamming it, and stood there glaring at me.

"There's a goldang crowd of people comin' in the lobby," he said.

"They wake you up, Harry?" I asked.

"Goldang it, Joe—I wasn't sleepin'."

"Give me odds on it?"

"Now look—"

"Okay, Harry—what do all the people want?"

"I don't know. Sam Heller's boy run in and said they's a crowd of people comin' to see Singer Batts. George Cooler's with 'em. There! They're comin' in. Hear?"

I heard. It sounded like quite a crowd.

"Please find out what they want, Joe," said Singer Batts.

It startled me. Singer had been reading all the time. I didn't know he'd even heard Harry.

"Sure," I said. "Go back out to the desk, Harry. I'll be right there."

Harry went to the door. He turned the knob and opened it. Then he closed it again and looked at me.

"Julia Stauffer's downstairs in the tavern, gettin' drunk," he said.

"What the hell has that got to do with anything?"

Harry blinked.

"Nothin', I guess."

"Go ahead, Harry. When we get through with the people, I'll take you downstairs and buy you a gallon of beer."

"Okay."

Harry went out. I looked at Singer.

"He said they wanted to see you."

"Yes," Singer said. "But I must finish this chapter. I can't stop in the middle of a marginal note. If you'll explain—"

"Sure," I said.

I opened the door and went into the lobby. Harry was sitting behind the desk, looking unhappy and sleepy but not daring to go to sleep.

There were about twenty of Preston's more or less solid citizens standing around. George Cooler was in the middle, looking worried and harassed. George was the town marshal—a big guy—wide in the shoulders with a badly roughed-up mug; tough on the outside, but inside as sensitive and innocent as a baby. Had a high sense of duty and not a hell of a lot of brains.

Closest to George were three examples of the better people in town. Two of them were women—which was undoubtedly what made George Cooler so nervous.

Mrs. Granger—whose first name really is Esmerelda—was Harley Granger's wife. Harley owned the hardware store and some property around town. I didn't like him or his family, especially his wife. They were the sanctimonious type and made up a big part of Preston's unorganized but potent "watch and ward" society.

Next to Mrs. Granger stood Mrs. Stephenson, whose husband owned a feed mill down by the bridge. She was in the same class with Mrs. Granger, but she wasn't so loud about it.

The third thorn in George Cooler's side was the Reverend Harold Albritton, of the Gospel Church. The parson was the hellfire and brimstone type, who every year took it on himself to clean up the carnival that the Eagles Club brought to town. Reverend Albritton would inspect the concessions and make recommendations to the Eagles as to which ones were likely to ruin the flower of our youth and ought to be closed. So the Eagles would run the kootch show and the chuck-a-luck table to hell out of town and everything in would be on the up and up again.

When I first saw Mrs. Stephenson and the preacher and Esmerelda Granger there with George Cooler, I couldn't figure out why they wanted to see Singer Batts. People of this ilk were a little suspicious of Singer—because he didn't go to church and he didn't get out and mingle, but spent most of his time reading old books and studying. They didn't have anything they could hang on him—he never committed any sins or indiscretions. But they were suspicious. They suspected he was a "philosopher"—a guy who doesn't work, who just thinks—always a loose character in a tight society.

(The reason I can explain all that is that Singer once explained it to me.)

The rest of the crowd was about half male and half female and it looked like they'd come along for the ride. Esmerelda looked grim and Mrs. Stephenson looked smug and the Reverend Albritton looked pious.

I looked at George Cooler.

"What's the trouble?" I asked him.

"It's about Linda Graves, Joe," he said. "Is Singer here?"

"He's here," I said. "He's busy right now. He wanted me to come out and see what you have on your minds. He'll be here pretty soon. In the meantime—anything I can do…"

Esmerelda Granger puffed up like a pigeon and threw out her big chest.

"This is ridiculous," she said. "There's nothing we need Singer Batts for. We simply want George Cooler to do his duty as our law officer."

"Exactly," said Mrs. Stephenson. "Isn't that right, Reverend Albritton?"

"Quite correct, Mrs. Stephenson," said the parson. "That is the whole thing reduced to its simplest terms."

George Cooler shoved a hand through his short hair.

"I ain't sure it's my duty," he said. "I told 'em I'd put it up to Singer Batts, being as I think Singer has got more brains than anybody else in town—"

Esmerelda puffed up a little more.

"I don't agree with that at all," she said.

"What particular duty do you want George to perform?" I asked her.

Mrs. Granger's jaws worked like an air hammer, pounding out the words.

"I want him to investigate the goings-on at the place."

I was surprised.

"Something going on out there?" I asked. "The way I heard it, nothing's going on."

"These people claim," George Cooler said, "that Linda Graves shut herself up in the old house and is carryin' on some dark thing."

"Some dark thing?" I looked at the parson. "That sounds like you."

The Reverend Albritton drew himself up.

"I believe that is the way I described it. It is our feeling that if reports are true, an investigation is certainly called for."

"What reports?" I asked.

"Several people have *seen* things at the place," said Esmerelda.

"What things?"

I was getting tired of this.

"Things," snapped Esmerelda.

"To be quite frank about it," the parson said, "people claim to have seen a man in the Graves place."

"Oh, God!" I said. "Men go in and out of houses, too. Just like women."

"At night," Mrs. Stephenson said.

"Late at night," said Esmerelda.

A voice in the back of the crowd said, "That's right!"

And somebody else said, "Roy Eldridge's boy saw him, too." Another voice said, "Is that so? I hadn't heard—" and then everybody was talking at once and I began to think about the guests on the second floor. I held up my hands, but it didn't help. The chatter got louder and louder.

"Shut up!" I yelled, and they did.

"Let's see if I've got this straight. Somebody saw a man in Linda Grave's house late at night. So you want George Cooler to go out there and investigate. Right?"

"In a rudimentary way, that's right," Esmerelda said.

"I think the whole thing is too damn rudimentary," I said. "What's George going to do, ask for a marriage license?"

"That would be the first step," the parson said.

I stared at him.

"Are you serious?" I asked.

"Look," said George Cooler. "I got no legal right to go bustin' into anybody's private life unless there's somethin' wrong."

"There's something wrong, all right," Esmerelda said.

"What if the guy's her husband?" I said.

"I don't believe it," Esmerelda said.

"You wouldn't believe it even if he proved it."

Her chest practically busted out of her foundation. She took a couple of steps toward me.

"You look here, Joe Spinder," she said, "you're not too well established as a member of this community yourself. I know my duties as a citizen and I won't put up with any interference from you. We didn't come here to see you, anyway."

A new voice from behind me said, "Did you come to see me, Mrs. Granger?"

It was Singer Batts. I hadn't heard him come out of the suite. I didn't know how long he'd been standing there.

Thin, tired in the face, slightly stooped, he shambled to the desk near where I stood and leaned against it, turning his bashful, slow smile on Esmerelda. I guess she hadn't seen him either. Her jaw snapped shut and she tossed her head like an angry mare and wouldn't look at either of us.

Singer looked at the people gathered in the lobby. He nodded to them, spoke to some and waved at somebody in the back. A man said, "Hi, Singer."

They all felt better now, with Singer there. Most people in town had confidence in him. He was like an oracle. Singer was too shy to admit this, but I think he felt it sometimes. I think this was one of the times.

"I overheard the burden of your complaint," he said talking straight to Esmerelda Granger. "Are you sure you want to investigate Linda Graves?"

Esmerelda had lost her patience.

"Now listen, Singer," she said. "You needn't try any of your high-toned arguments with me. Maybe you know a lot about Shakespeare—but I'm a responsible citizen of this town and I know my rights. I want—"

Singer was smiling—not in a sarcastic way, but just enough to be friendly.

"Sometimes," he said, "people assume rights that they don't really have. Maybe this is one of the times."

"Every respectable citizen," said the Reverend Albritton, "has a right to make certain that his children are developing in a moral atmosphere. I feel—"

Singer overlooked the Reverend Albritton. His gaze wandered to some of the other people in the crowd and he started to talk to all of them, not just Esmerelda Granger.

"The Graves family," he said, "was an honored group in our community. No finer man than Seth Graves ever lived. Seth's wife was a fine woman. Linda Graves was a bright, honest girl, who looked every man and woman straight in the eye and spoke her true thoughts. I think you all know that."

It was very quiet in the lobby now. Singer, as usual, had got hold of them. I knew he wouldn't let go until he'd had his say.

"Therefore," he went on, "we have no cause automatically to become suspicious of Linda."

Mrs. Stephenson couldn't hold off any longer.

"How do you know what she did after she left town," she said, "more than twenty years ago—?"

Singer shook his head.

"I don't know," he said. "I think it is probably not any of our affair. You all knew and loved Linda Graves. If you stop to think about that, you'll admit it. You have no reason now to turn against her. Someone has seen a light in her house—very late at night. Someone else has seen, or thought he's seen a man in her house. If out of these things you plan to build a case for police investigation, then you must surely be hard put to it for something to occupy your time."

A man in the back said loudly, "Singer's right, by golly!"

Esmerelda's voice was bitter.

"'Singer's right.' Oh yes—Singer's always right. But when decent, church-going people try to assume a little responsibility for the community—"

"Don't you mean a little responsibility for living other people's lives?" Singer said. "I think I know what has caused all this. I think it's plain curiosity—inquisitiveness. I think perhaps you are a little piqued because Linda Graves hasn't shown herself in town. You want all the information there is—where she's been, what she's done, how many marriages, how many divorces—. And to satisfy your curiosity, you will take any steps that occur to you."

"That's not true at all!" screamed Esmerelda.

"I think it's true," Singer said. "I suggest that you have every right to satisfy that curiosity, if you can. A friendly call on Linda Graves, to welcome her home—"

"She won't let anybody in," Mrs. Stephenson said. "She talks through the door."

Singer's smile was beautiful to see.

"So," he said. "She has a right to talk through her own door. If she refuses to talk to you, you insist she's a criminal. You have no case here. Your private investigations are your own business. But I warn you not to send George Cooler out there. It would be unfriendly, it probably would be fruitless and certainly it would be unconstitutional."

George Cooler stood straight on his own two gams and said, "Singer is right. I ain't goin'."

Esmerelda Granger glared at him. She glared at Singer and at me. Then she turned, with her chin in the air, and marched out of the lobby. Mrs. Stephenson minced after her, and the Reverend Albritton, with pious head shaking, followed. Slowly the crowd broke up and drifted out. George Cooler came up and grabbed Singer's hand.

"That was a good job, Singer," he said. "I knew I didn't have no right to do a thing like that."

Singer smiled.

"You were right, George. Don't let people push you into sticking your fingers in a trap."

"That damn Granger woman," George said. "There's somethin' about her. I get fussed—"

"Mrs. Granger," Singer said, "lives a narrow life, regrets it can't be broader and chafes at the thought of those for whom it is broader—if they make it that way."

"Yes, sir!" George said. "I gotta be goin'. Thanks, Singer. You sure done me a good turn."

He went out.

"Come in and sit down, Joe," Singer said. "I've got to tell you a story."

I followed him into the suite.

CHAPTER TWO

Singer settled down in his Boston rocker and started right in.

"A good many years ago," he said, "there was a girl in Preston named Linda Graves."

"Seems like I've heard," I said.

"Linda Graves was a beautiful, high-spirited girl. Some people thought she was a little wild and independent, and didn't quite approve of her—but they couldn't help liking her. There was never anything malicious spoken of Linda Graves."

"Sounds a little dull."

"On the contrary, Joseph. I am not saying that the smoke of malicious talk lacked fire to cause it. There was plenty of fire. The thing I am saying is that there was practically no smoke."

"All right."

"I cannot account for this. I only say it was the case. It may have been that the fire of Linda Graves burned so brightly and consumed so much of what it fed on that nothing was left for smoke."

I looked at him.

"Will you please do that once more—?"

"It doesn't matter. I am trying to show you what kind of girl Linda Graves was."

"Something so hot she didn't have to smoke—or something—"

"We'll let it go at that, Joe."

"Yes, sir. And quite right, too."

"Many young men in town fell in love with Linda. They swarmed about her. Some she encouraged, some she played with, some she spurned. A few of them—nobody knows how many, or who they were—she loved. And I have heard it said that to have been loved by Linda Graves—"

I guess my mouth was hanging open. Singer stopped and stared at me, a funny look on his face.

"Yes, Joe?" he said.

"Excuse me—but I'm having a hard time hooking this up. You talk like you were writing a book. How do you know all this stuff? Were you one of them—one of these guys she loved?"

He sort of drew himself up.

"At that time," he said, "I was approximately ten years old."

I took another drink.

"Well," I said, "let's go on with the story. I'll try not to interrupt."

"I don't mind the interruptions. It's that constant look of amazement on your face."

"Try not looking at me."

"That will be a pleasure."

"Oh, the hell with it. Go ahead."

"Very well. As I say—everybody loved Linda. There was something about her—something none of the other girls had."

I suppressed myself.

"She had a far-off quality about her—something wild, like an animal. It was as though she had paused in Preston only for a time—say for the season—as though she were here by accident and in the next year would be somewhere else—in some other pasture."

"Pasture?"

There was a long pause. Finally Singer said, "My dear Joseph. There are many things about you I admire. I have a greater respect for your talents—such as they are—than for those of any other citizen I know. In some ways I might almost be said to love you, as a man loves a brother. But that I must account to you for the accuracy and forcefulness of my speech, for the manner in which I express myself—that I deny."

I drank my drink and kept my mouth shut. I guess it was high time.

"By this time you will have understood—I hope—that Linda Graves was not a personality who would fit into the routine life of Preston. She wanted something else. And she had enough character to go after what she wanted.

"She left Preston. And it was the manner of her going and the length of her absence that gives this story its point. She said no good-bys, she visited no one to make any farewells. She bought no ticket on the train. She simply went away. One day she was here, laughing, talking, seen on the street. The next day she was gone. Gone as completely, as finally, as though she had never been. And nobody ever saw her in Preston again—nobody, until a few days ago, when she came back to her father's house. Apparently nobody has actually seen her yet. But people say she has come back."

I still kept my mouth shut. Probably because I couldn't think of anything to say. The story was getting pretty good.

Singer Batts looked out the window. There isn't much to see out of our window—the side of the harness shop, which is yellow brick, and if you strain your neck you see a little triangle of light that shows up some storefronts across the street. But Singer spent a lot of time looking out. Of course, Singer did a lot of thinking.

I had finished my drink. I set the glass down.

"What did you want me to do?" I asked.

He didn't answer right away. When he did it was in a voice so quiet I had to strain to hear.

"I'm worried, Joe. About Linda Graves. I feel a certain responsibility for her—for reasons I will explain shortly. I want to make sure she's all right, that if there's something she needs, she's getting it. I'm worried because she's back—or everyone's saying she's back and yet she hasn't appeared. That's not like Linda Graves. I'm worried about what has happened to her."

I waited. After a while he said, "I want you to go out and see her."

"Me?"

"Yes. I want you to go out there as a friendly neighbor, talk to her, try to find out whether she needs anything."

"But she never heard of me. I never knew her. Why would she talk to me?"

"I think she'd talk to you before she'd talk to anyone who had known her. If she has shut herself away, it's for a reason and she's a willful and stubborn character. I don't think she'd let any of the old natives in. I can only imagine that some serious trouble has come to her and I want to help her. But I don't think she'd see me any more than she'd see anybody else."

"You think she might see me?"

"Yes."

"You want me just to go out there, say, 'Hi, Linda, I'm Joe Spinder. What's wrong, baby?'"

"You're not far wrong at that."

"And you think that'll break her down?"

"I don't know. But nobody else has been able even to set eyes on her. It's worth trying."

"I'll do it," I said. "I don't have much hope for it, but I'll do it. I promised Harry some beer. I'll get him fixed up and then go out to the Graves place."

I reached for my hat and found the keys to my car.

"By the way," I said at the door. "Why all the concern?" There was another pause, while Singer gazed out the window.

"My mother died when I was a child," he said.

"I know."

"You remember I told you that many men loved Linda Graves, but that she returned this love only to a few?"

"Yeah."

"One of those few was my father."

"Oh."

"Just before my father died, over ten years after Linda Graves had gone away, he asked me to see that if she ever came back or if I ever ran into her anywhere, to see that she was taken care of, that she was all right and lacked for nothing."

"I get it."

"It was the only deathbed promise my father exacted. Since he was the kind of man he was, he requested it seriously and after much thought. It was no dying fancy. He meant it."

"Okay," I said. "I'll go see her."

I went out and got Harry Baird and we went downstairs to the tavern.

CHAPTER THREE

The tavern was a new addition. We'd rented the space under the lobby of the hotel—a sort of basement—to Frank Cervasi. Frank sold beer and wine. There was no hard liquor license in Preston, except for package goods.

Frank tried to keep a quiet, clean place, but he didn't have much help. Still, it wasn't bad. He had a few tables and a little bar and two booths. His patrons were mostly guys who worked at the roofing factory or the condensary and in shops around town. Once in a while some couple dropped in after a show, as did the traveling men who stopped at the hotel regularly. Also—Julia Stauffer.

Julia was there now. Harry and I sat down at the bar and Julia Stauffer was two stools away from me. There were a couple of other people—guys I didn't know well enough to speak to and on the stool next to Julia, Jim Dennis.

Jim Dennis had a plumbing business. He was a big, slightly flabby guy, with black, bristly hair—all over. Behind his back, people sometimes called him "the ape." His face was a little like an ape, too, and always glum. I never saw him smile. He sat there now beside Julia Stauffer, drinking his beer—half a glass per swallow—looking glum.

Julia Stauffer was maybe forty-eight years old. Sometimes she looked sixty—sometimes thirty-five. She was big and a little flabby now and her face was lined and freckled. She had long black hair which she did up on top of her head and her full lips were very red. She was the wife of Frank Stauffer, one of Preston's two attorneys.

Harry and I ordered beers and minded our own business—or tried to. Julia wouldn't let us. I was sitting closest to her and the first thing I knew, she was on the stool next to mine and her arm was around my neck.

"Joe, honey," she said. "What was all the fuss up in your lobby?"

"A delegation of citizens," I said. "Something about Linda Graves."

"Linda Graves?"

"Yeah—Linda Graves. Remember—?"

She took her arm away from around my neck.

"You son of a bitch," she said.

"Sorry," I said.

"Fill this up, Frank," Julia said, pushing her glass across the bar. It was a beer glass. Frank filled it up with muscatel. I shuddered.

"Listen," Julia said, "is your boyfriend, Singer, going to look into the mystery of the Graves place?"

"There's a mystery?" I said.

"There's always been a mystery about the Graves place."

"I don't want to discuss it especially," I said.

"Oh—you don't?"

"Uh-uh."

She threw back her big head and laughed and looked at Jim Dennis.

"He doesn't want to discuss it," she said.

You were always patient with Julia Stauffer, because you liked her husband Frank. But I didn't feel very patient right now. I didn't have time.

"Look," I said, "I'd just as soon discuss Linda Graves herself."

She gave me that dirty look again, finished her wine and got onto her feet.

"To hell with you, Joe Spinder," she said and went out. I looked at Jim Dennis.

"There's nothing wrong at the Graves place," he said.

"That's what I figured," I said.

"Be a waste of time foolin' around out there. If Linda Graves wants to be alone—then leave her alone."

"Sure."

"I heard those old biddies chattering up there in the lobby," he said. "If my wife ever carried on like that, I'd take a strap to her."

"I hope that won't be necessary."

"It better not be."

"You didn't want to fight with me about it, did you?" Jim didn't answer.

"Harry, get on back to the desk," I said. "I've got to run a little errand."

"Sure, Joe."

"And try to stay awake."

"Oh, now, Joe—"

"All right, Harry."

We got up. Harry went upstairs into the lobby and I got in my car. Just as I got it started and pulled away from the curb, Jim Dennis came out, crossed the street and got in his car.

* * * *

I drove north on the county road, along the creek. It was a nice day, sunny and warm but not hot. There was a breeze and kids were swimming in the creek.

The Graves place sat on a big hill at the north edge of town. There were no other houses close to it and the hill was overgrown with shrubs and old, decaying trees. There was a high iron fence surrounding the lot, stretching for a quarter of a mile along the road and leading back up and over the hill. Grass grew high and gray along the fence, both inside and out. A rutted, winding drive led up to the house.

I turned in between the two stone pillars with the old-fashioned lanterns on top. I turned in, took a look at the drive and stopped. Tires were hard to get.

I pulled the car over, turned off the motor and got out. Getting out I bumped my head against the top of the door, knocking my hat off. I picked up the hat, threw it onto the seat and slammed the door. My temper never was one to stand up under stuff like that.

Then I turned back to the drive and walked up toward the house. It was quite a climb and I was winded when I reached the porch.

The house was in bad shape. A lot of settling and shifting had gone on underneath it and the porch was sagging. One of the pillars that supported the porch roof was rotted through at the bottom. The steps were worn and loose and there was a broken pane in the ornamental window beside the doorframe.

The bell was an old-fashioned pull thing that rang way deep inside the house. I rang, waited, rang again. After the third ring I heard footsteps. They came closer, then stopped, as if whoever had come had hesitated just on the other side of the door and was waiting.

So I waited, and nothing happened.

I knocked. There was only silence. I didn't hear anyone moving away.

"Miss Graves?" I said loudly.

After a moment a voice came from the other side of the door.

"Yes?"

It was a strong, well-cultivated voice, a little sharp around the edges, a little impatient, but the voice of a gal who knew her own mind.

"I'm Joe Spinder," I said.

Another moment and the voice said, "What do you want?"

"I'd like to talk to you. I'm on a friendly errand."

"I don't remember the name."

"You never knew me," I said. "I'm a newcomer to Preston."

After another, longer pause, the doorknob turned and the door opened a little. I stood there.

"May I come in?" I said.

The door opened a little wider.

"Yes," the voice said, and I stepped into the vestibule of the old house. A woman stood there. But it was so dark I couldn't see much of her. She didn't say anything more and I was trying to figure out my next move and didn't say anything cither. By peering intently in the direction of the voice, I could make out her general appearance. She was tall and slender—not skinny. I figured her hair to be blonde. She stood very straight.

I peered at her, wishing she'd turn on a light.

"Why did you come?" she asked suddenly.

It startled me, threw me off balance.

"Why—I just wanted to make sure you were all right," I said. "Nobody in town had seen you, and people were wondering how you were, and I thought maybe since I was a stranger—you'd be a little freer in talking to me."

"I'm quite all right," she said. "I haven't seen anybody because I want to rest and be quiet. I will come into town when I feel more like it."

"Oh, sure," I said. "I don't want to intrude on you. Truth is, it was Singer Batts who asked me to come out here."

"I see."

She didn't offer anything more, and finally I said, "If you're all right, I'll run along. Just remember—if there's anything you need any time, let us know. Singer will do anything you ask. And so will I."

"Thank you," she said.

I backed out the door, saying something silly that I can't remember now, and she closed it and there I stood on the porch.

As I walked back down the drive toward the car I thought how dull I had been and how I probably hadn't accomplished anything. I hated to tell Singer I hadn't found out anything. On the other hand, I had got inside the house. That was better than anybody else had done.

I opened the car door, reached in to pick up my hat and sat down behind the wheel. There was a slip of white paper sticking up out of the hat band.

I pulled the paper out and put the hat on my head. The paper was folded once. I opened it and read,

"If you value your life stay away from Linda Graves."

It sounded a little silly at first glance and I read it again. The message was printed crudely with a dull pencil. Looked like a kid's writing. I stuck it in my pocket, turned on the ignition and let my foot rest on the starter. Then I turned off the ignition, opened the door and climbed out of the car. I made the trip up to the house again, climbed the porch steps and rang the bell.

We went through the whole thing all over, only this time she didn't open the door.

"Look, Miss Graves," I said, "when I went back to my car I found something you ought to know about. I'm worried about you."

"What did you find?"

"A warning."

"Warning me, or you?"

"Me."

"Well?"

"I have a feeling you're in danger, Miss Graves."

"I haven't had any warning."

"I think this was intended for you as well as for me."

"Please don't trouble yourself. I'm quite all right."

"I think I ought to stick around and—well, see that nothing happens."

"No. Please go away. I can take care of myself."

"I don't doubt it," I said, "but I have a certain responsibility."

"I won't stand here and argue about it," she said. "Please go."

"Well—all right," I said.

I went down off the porch slowly, thinking: The hell with it! If she's so stubborn, let her take care of herself.

I knew that wasn't the right attitude, but I couldn't figure out any way around it. I got in the car and backed out of the drive.

A few feet down the road, headed north, Julia Stauffer sat in their Buick sedan. She seemed to be having trouble starting it. I stopped opposite her and leaned out. Her heavy, gaudy face was flushed. I wouldn't have let her drive my car.

"Trouble?" I said.

"Damn thing won't start. Give me a push, Joe. It's the lousy battery."

"Sure," I said.

I went on, backed and turned on the narrow road, came up behind her and got our bumpers together. It was a heavy car and she must have had it in low gear. It was all I could do to move it. But it caught quickly and she gunned it and went off up the road. I turned in at the Graves gate, backed out to get headed toward town and drove back to the hotel.

Singer was sitting in the lobby, talking to some local loafer. I went in, nodded and stopped at the desk. Everything was running along all right, we had two vacancies and were expecting a couple of salesmen later, so that would be taken care of. Nothing unpleasant had happened—with one exception. As I leaned across the desk, Harry reached underneath and pulled out a special delivery letter. He handed it to me and I glanced at the return address.

Just as I thought.

The letter was addressed to Singer. Feeling like a crook, I snaked it into my pocket. I didn't like the way Harry was looking at me. I stared back at him hard and he shrugged and looked away.

"Listen," I said, "if any word of this correspondence gets out—I'll know why."

"I ain't sayin' anything," Harry said.

"Okay. And none of this nonsense about me interfering with the U. S mail either."

"Sure, Joe."

"All right."

I went on into the suite and took off my hat. After a couple of minutes Singer came in. He went over to his rocker by the window, sat down and waited.

I told him about it, everything, word for word, footstep for footstep. When I'd finished he sat looking out the window.

"Let me see the note you found," he said.

I handed it to him. He read it, then he sat holding it, gazing out the window.

"Looks like a childish prank," he said.

"Yeah."

"But what if it isn't? What if Linda is in real danger?"

"I don't know. She won't let anybody come in. I could go up and prowl around the house all night, like a watchman. But if she should find out about it—"

"No. That wouldn't do. The local police are—or I should say, 'is'—out of the question."

"Either way you say it, it's true, brother."

"Linda was an expert shot, with pistol or rifle. She knows how to take care of herself. I can only conclude that if she is in trouble it is not something she would admit to anyone and perhaps she is best left alone."

"That seems to be the way she wants it."

"Then for now, Joe, that's the way it will be."

I reached in my pocket and pulled out the special delivery letter. I had never meant not to give it to him, of course. I just wanted him to realize I knew when he got them. It was the only bad habit he had and I wanted to help him break it.

Singer thinks he ought to settle down with a good woman—somebody who'll take an interest in his studies and keep the place tidied up, and so on. But he can't stand the thought of coming right out and asking a woman to marry him, especially any woman in Preston. He shies away from them like a horse from trains. He thinks he can do it by mail.

So he writes to these lonely heart agencies. He gets some of the weirdest letters and pictures. It would be funny and I wouldn't pay any attention to it if it weren't for the fact that someday he might really get hooked.

I handed him the letter.

"Came a little while ago," I said. "I forgot to give it to you."

He looked at me, then at the letter and right away that guilty look came to his face. He started to open the envelope, then stopped and looked at me again.

"You consider this my chief vice, don't you, Joe?"

"I consider it your only vice."

"I think you're sincere. I might as well admit also that way deep inside, I have the feeling you're right."

I waited.

"Therefore," he said, "I will make a determined effort to break this habit—beginning now."

He tore the unopened letter into several pieces and dropped it in the wastebasket beside his chair.

"Congratulations," I said and decided to let well enough alone.

* * * *

We ate dinner then, me having to argue with Singer to get him to drink some coffee, at least, and eat a piece of bread. Singer never eats unless he's forced into it. Never saw anything like it. Doesn't seem to feel the need of either food or sleep. I don't know how he lives.

After dinner I went to a movie, came home, drank a few beers and went to bed. Singer was sitting in his rocker, reading.

CHAPTER FOUR

About three o'clock in the morning I woke up. Singer was standing over my bed, calling me softly. Probably had been standing there for fifteen minutes. He won't do anything so rough as to shake anyone. He just starts talking and waits patiently for the awakening.

I blinked, turned over on my back, sat up.

"Yeah?" I said.

"I have just received a telephone call," he said, "from Esmerelda Granger. She said that Ernie Seton, who lives across the road from the Graves place, called her to say that he'd seen someone prowling around there a little while ago."

"Yeah?"

"While I put no stock in Mrs. Granger's somewhat libidinous imagination, I have a feeling. It is a feeling that will keep me awake."

"What kind of a feeling?"

"I must see and speak to Linda Graves. If I have to force my way in, I'll have to do it. Will you drive me out there?"

"Now?"

"Now."

"Okay. Let me throw on some old rag—"

I got up and dressed. Singer was waiting for me in the living room of the suite. He was standing up instead of sitting in the rocker. That meant he was a little impatient.

We got in the car and drove out to the Graves place. There was such a bright moon I could have driven the county road without any lights. But after we turned in at the gateposts and got out of the car the moonlight wasn't much good. The growth of trees and shrubs and weeds was so thick that the moonlight couldn't get through. We had to feel our way along the ruts of the drive.

We'd walked about ten steps when I grabbed Singer's arm. He stopped.

"If she really is expecting trouble," I said, "and hears somebody prowling around the place, she's likely to take a shot at us."

"We'll be as quiet as possible. It's a chance we'll have to take."

It was not a chance I enjoyed taking.

We climbed on up slowly to the house. There were no lights inside or any sound. That was natural enough at 3:30 a.m. But standing there with little skinny wisps of moonlight leaking through, looking at the old, faded house and remembering the conversation I'd had with its owner, I began to have a "feeling" too. It was a prickly feeling that started in the back of my neck and wound up in my stomach.

Singer looked at the old house, started toward the porch and stopped.

"Shouldn't wake her, if she's sleeping," he said. "Let's take a turn around the place."

"Let's keep our eyes open," I said.

"Of course."

We walked around the southwest corner of the house and back toward the old barn that stood off the southeast corner. Once in a while we'd pass an open space in the trees and bushes and the moonlight would come through suddenly, lighting up the ground and a piece of the wall of the house. The first couple of times it made me jump. Then I got used to it.

Singer shambled ahead of me, his head turning now and then to the house, now and then toward the foliage on our right.

At the back corner he paused. He looked at the back door of the house, then went toward the barn.

It was a small barn that had been used for harness, buggies and livery long ago. There were a couple of stalls in it for horses. There hadn't been any horses in it for years.

The door was closed and Singer felt around till he found a chain that dangled as far down as his shoulder.

He pulled the chain and I got hold of the edge of the big door. The hinges were rusty. When I pulled on the door it squeaked like a stepped-on puppy. I stopped pulling and held it.

"That'll do it," I said under my breath.

"It sounds louder than it is," Singer said.

"You don't mind if I get behind it and push?"

"Not at all. Just open it."

I pushed the door open. It squealed some more, but not as loudly as at first and after I had it open and listened for a minute, nothing happened.

We went in and I lit a match. I got my hand all tangled up in cobwebs, dropped the match, stepped on it, brushed off my hand and found another match.

"Nobody's been in here for a long time," I said.

"Apparently not."

Singer stood just inside the door, peering through the dark into the barn. There were shadows of old bits of harness and some buggy wheels. In one corner there was an old trunk. The smell of the place was thick and heavy with dust and you could tell that the mice had built a young city in it.

Singer was talking to himself.

"I used to have a wonderful time playing in this old barn."

I looked at him in the glow of a match.

"With Linda Graves?" I asked.

"With Linda Graves' horses."

I threw down the match, stepped on it.

"Come on," I said, "I've got the creeps already."

I stepped outside. Singer followed me and I pushed the door to as softly as possible.

Singer turned and walked past the back corner of the house to the back porch. It was a deep, screened porch, but the screening had decayed and there were big holes in it. I wondered why nobody had ever bought the Graves place, or taken care of it.

We started on past the porch toward the north side of the house. Then Singer stopped suddenly, so that I bumped into him and rubbed my nose against his coat. He turned back, went to the porch, opened the outer screen door and looked in.

"Why would she leave the door open?" he said.

I looked. The inner door, between the house and the porch was standing open.

"Don't think she would," I said.

"No."

Singer stepped onto the porch and went over to the open kitchen door. I followed. Every board creaked. I wanted a drink and I promised myself a big one as soon as we got back to the hotel.

Singer peered into the kitchen. It gave me about the same feeling as I'd had looking at the barn, only there weren't any cobwebs.

"We're going in," Singer whispered. "I don't like the look of things. I don't want to disturb Linda, but I want to check up on things. I'm more familiar with the house than you are. You take the first floor and I'll take the back stairs that lead up from the kitchen. Go straight out of the kitchen into the dining room. There are two doors on your right, one in the dining room, one in the front parlor. There's a small sitting room off the parlor, a bedroom off the dining room, lake your time. There's no hurry. Don't light a match unless you have to. If you find anything unusual, call me."

"You think I won't?"

"Very well. I'll meet you right here."

"Yeah? Don't be funny. You're going upstairs and crawl back into the wall, along with Linda's horses and all the other ghosts around this place."

"Levity," Singer said, "should be reserved for the daylight hours."

"My God!" I said. "How do you think I manage to keep going?"

Singer was gone. He'd stepped into the kitchen and disappeared. I listened carefully, heard the dull shuffle of his feet on the back stairs.

I had a horrible hatred for this damned house.

I went into the kitchen, straining my eyes, trying to figure out which direction would lead me to the dining room. I ignored Singer's advice and struck a match. Directly ahead of me was a swinging door. It was closed. It would lead either to the dining room or to that place where guys like me can probably expect to wind up someday—if anywhere at all.

I shook out the match, dropped it on the floor and went through the swinging door.

The dining room was big and empty. The furniture had probably been sold off. There were a couple of chairs against the wall, but nothing else. The windows were shuttered but a little moonlight filtered through the slats—enough to show me the door on my right, leading to a bedroom. I started over there, then stopped and headed on through the dining room toward the parlor. The bedroom could wait.

There was a little more furniture in the parlor, but not much. Here the windows were shuttered, too, but on the north side, where the foliage was not so thick, there was more moonlight and I got a pretty good view of the room. There was nothing unusual in it—except maybe me.

I went over to the door that Singer had said led into a small sitting room. I opened it carefully. It was black as carbon paper. I struck another match. It looked as if all the furniture from the other rooms had been thrown in here. Stuff was piled all over. There were tables, chairs, bookcases, a couple of trunks. I held the match close to the top of one of the tables. It was thick with dust, not a mark on it. I backed out and closed the door.

Across the room I saw the vestibule where I had stood the night before, talking to Linda Graves. I went over there. A woman's tweed coat hung on a hanger beside a full-length mirror. There were several hooks, but there was only the one coat. No hat. Nothing else to show that anybody lived in the house.

Maybe, I thought, nobody does. Maybe I didn't—

Then I decided not to think about that.

There was only one place left I hadn't explored. The bedroom. I stood still for a minute, listening. Once in a while I could hear the sounds of Singer's footsteps upstairs. I was glad to hear them.

I went back into the dining room and up to the door of the bedroom. I gripped the knob hard, turned it very slowly. It seemed as if I turned it for an hour. Then the door swung free. I pushed it open.

There were no shutters in this room, it was flooded with moonlight. I didn't have to strike a match to see that Linda Graves was in bed. I backed out, pulled the door to, let the knob turn back silently.

No, she wasn't cither in bed, I thought. She was on the bed. Not in it.

Reluctantly, I opened the door again, looked. I went over to the bed. She was lying on the bed, on her side. She wore a long flowered dressing gown and slippers.

"Miss Graves," I said. Then louder, "Miss Graves!"

There was no answer. I touched her shoulder, shook her gently.

"Miss Graves!"

There was a lamp on a small bedside table. I switched it on. Linda Graves lay peacefully on her side, apparently asleep. Only trouble with it was, her eyes were open. Some people sleep with their eyes open—but not often. I looked at her eyes. They were open, but they were not looking at anything. They were dull and the pupils were not exactly round. She would not be looking at anything again.

I heard steps on the back stairs. Singer was coming down. He had shown a great attachment to Linda Graves. I hated to have him walk in on this without any warning.

I went out of the room and pushed through the swinging door. I met him just as he came down off the last step. "Find anything?" I asked.

"Nothing. Did you?"

"Look," I said, "I came out here to slow you down. Don't take it too hard."

"What is it?"

"It's your girlfriend, Linda Graves."

"She's sleeping in the downstairs bedroom, then."

"She's dead."

"Dead?"

"Yeah."

"Are you sure?"

"Positive. Sorry to break it so suddenly. But I didn't want you walking in on it."

He said nothing for a while. Then he passed his hand slowly over his face.

"I have a horror of looking at the face of death," he said. "I ought to take your word for it, call the doctor. But—"

"Anything you say."

"Where is she?"

"In the bedroom."

I turned and went back through the swinging door to the bedroom. Singer followed me. His steps dragged. It was plain he didn't want to. Something was pushing him—something from twenty years back.

I went to the foot of the bed. Singer stepped past me, went to the little table where the lamp stood. He looked down. Then he stopped and looked at her face. He straightened slowly, turned and looked at me. His head was shaking slowly back and forth.

"Sorry," I said. "I should have stayed this aft—"

"Joe," he said, in a strange voice. "This is not Linda Graves."

CHAPTER FIVE

There was a considerable silence. I couldn't think of anything to say.

Then Singer said, "I have no idea who this is, and I'm sorry for her. But it's not Linda Graves. Is it the woman you spoke to yesterday afternoon?"

"How do I know? Whoever it is—she was alive then."

"None of the talk around town has mentioned more than one woman."

"Everybody took it for granted it would be Linda Graves."

"Yes. And so did I."

"You're sure it's not Linda Graves?"

"I'd swear it."

"Been twenty years."

"Yes—but—Linda Graves—you don't understand."

"Okay," I said, "it isn't Linda Graves. But who is it?"

"I never saw her before."

"Hadn't we better get Doc Blanc?"

"Of course. Did you notice a telephone?"

"No."

"It isn't likely she'd have one put in. If she was the total stranger she seems to be, she wouldn't have wanted anybody to come in."

I went back into the parlor and dining room and into the vestibule. No telephone. I went back to the bedroom. "No phone," I said.

"You'd better drive into town and get Doc Blane. I'll stay here."

"The doc will hate me."

"He'll grumble, but he'll come."

"I don't know that *I* will."

"I can ride back with the doctor."

"I'm kidding," I said. "I want to know who this dead lady is."

I went out the front door, found my way down the drive to the car and headed toward town. It was after four-thirty now and there was some light in the east. I drove fast into town, turned east on Front Street and drove three blocks to Doc Blane's house. I knew he slept in a bedroom at the back of the house, so I went back there and tapped on his window. It took quite a lot of tapping. Then I heard him roll out of bed and come over to the window.

"What is it?" he asked.

"Joe Spinder. Can you come out and make an examination?"

"But listen," he said, "I delivered a baby only two hours ago. I'm trying to get a little sleep."

"Who had a baby, doc?"

"Liz Smith, down by the bridge. Boy. Eight and three-quarters pounds. Very hard job. Very big boy. Very small—well. It was tough—nerve-racking."

"Sorry," I said. "But Singer and I—"

"Is Singer sick, Joe?"

"No. It's a woman, and she's not sick. She's dead."

"If she's dead she can wait a little longer."

Doc pushed down the window and went away. I heard the bedsprings creak. I stood there swearing softly to myself. Suddenly the window flew open.

"Did you say she's dead?"

"I think she is. But I'm not officially qualified to say."

"All right. Give me a few minutes."

I waited outside the window. After a few minutes the back door opened and Doc Blanc came out, brushing the sleep out of his eyes, carrying his bag.

"My car's out in front," I said.

"I'll drive mine. Can't ever tell."

"All right. It's out at the Graves place."

Doc stopped, grabbed my arm.

"Joe! Is it Linda Graves?"

"Singer says no."

"Then who?"

I shrugged. "We don't know. Maybe you'll know after you see her."

I got in my car and doc backed his out of the drive and we went down Front Street again and out north toward the Graves place. Once or twice doc tooted his horn and I speeded up.

It was a lot lighter now and we didn't have any trouble with stumbling around in the ruts of the drive.

Inside the house doc said, "Where is she?"

"In the bedroom. Straight ahead."

Doc hurried back there and I followed. In the bedroom Singer was waiting. Looked as if he hadn't moved all the time I'd been gone.

"What's this, Singer?" Doc Blanc asked.

"I don't know," Singer said. "Do you know this woman?" Doc stooped and looked at her face. He shook his head. "She's dead, of course," Singer said.

Doc went through the motions.

"She's dead."

"For how long?" asked Singer.

"Can't tell very closely," doc said. "Maybe an hour, maybe two or three."

"Heart attack, perhaps?"

"Maybe."

Doc was loosening the front of the dressing gown. His long, thin fingers were busy, but his white head kept shaking slowly back and forth and his eyes darted around the room. He was puzzled. And he was not alone.

"Look here, Singer!" he said suddenly.

Singer and I bent over him. He had lifted the dead woman's chin and was looking at her neck. I saw a faint bluish mark, running across her throat and back upward under her ears.

Doc was looking at Singer.

"Strangled," he said.

He let her head drop back to the bed, closed up the dressing gown. He drew a blanket up from the foot of the bed and covered her. He stood up.

"It's a matter for the county officials," he said. Then his eyes twinkled a little. "Unless you've got it figured out already."

"I?" said Singer. "Nothing of the sort. I've not even made an attempt. I didn't realize there was anything to figure out—except her identity."

"Here's a purse," I said. I'd seen it lying on a chair near the bed. "Maybe there's something in here that'll tell us—"

"I looked," Singer said. "There's nothing.

I looked, too, just to be looking. There was some bills in the purse, a total of $366 and some change. There was a small pad of plain paper in a leather holder with a pencil attached. There was a package of cigarettes, half gone, and a pack of matches. I looked at the matches. They advertised the "7-11 Club" on North Sheridan Road, Chicago.

I closed the purse and put it back where I'd found it. "You didn't find any luggage around, any railway tickets?" asked Doc Blane.

"No," Singer said. "Of course, we haven't ransacked the house. I was interested in Linda Graves. This is someone else."

"It can't be Linda," doc said. "Linda was not so tall, and she was heavier, her arms and legs were bigger."

What memories, I thought. That must have been some girl, that Linda Graves.

"I'd better drive back to town," doc said, "and call the sheriff in Montpelier."

"You'd better not fail to tell George Cooler," I said.

As I've said, George was solid and dependable. But he was sensitive. He wouldn't like to be by-passed even by murder.

"I'll tell George, too," doc said. "But I hate to think of this getting all over town so fast. People will bother me to death asking questions."

"George will keep his mouth shut," I said, "if you mention it."

"Doctor," Singer said, "isn't Frank Stauffer the executor of the Graves estate?"

"I believe he is."

"He'd know positively whether or not this is Linda Graves."

"He would. He was closer to the family than anyone else in town. I'm sure it's not Linda myself. But Frank could certainly put it beyond doubt."

"He might, just possibly, be able to throw some light on this woman's identity," Singer said.

"It can't be the housing shortage," I said. "She's no vagrant."

"Suppose," Singer said to doc, "you stop by Frank's house and ask him to run out here. Joe and I will wait. I'd like to get this definitely established."

"Sure, I will," doc said. "I'm curious myself."

Doc picked up his bag and went out. I looked at Singer.

"She was murdered," I said.

"Yes."

"I haven't noticed any strangers in town."

"You are saying that she was killed by someone in Preston?"

"Not in so many words."

Singer shrugged his thin shoulders.

"We'll let the sheriff take care of the investigation, Joe."

"What if the sheriff needs a little help?"

"He's a capable sheriff. I don't think he'll need help." He was a capable sheriff, all right. He was a former city policeman and he was patient and thorough. He'd taken over criminal investigation for the county after the defeat of District Attorney Weaver in the last election. Weaver had been an impossible stuffed shirt. The new D. A had turned it all over to the sheriff and Sheriff Whitley was all right.

"But what if he does need help?" I persisted.

"If he should require some help," Singer said slowly, "I am bound to assist where I can. You know that I hate even the thought of murder and dislike having anything to do with it."

"Oh, sure," I said, "until you get your nose on a scent."

"When forced into it, Joseph, I try to make the best of it."

That was a he, but I let it pass. Singer is a natural sleuth. He's just inclined that way. But he has such a great reluctance to get mixed up in a murder that it amounts to a mental block. He has to be talked into it, or pushed. Once he's started, you can't tear him away.

"We'll see what happens when the sheriff comes," I said.

"You didn't notice any sort of luggage in the house, Joe, when you were looking around?"

"Nothing—except some old trunks in that sitting room off the parlor."

"I wonder who this woman is. I wonder why she came to be in the old Graves house. If the place had been sold, everybody in town would have known it."

"Maybe she was a friend of Linda's, coming back to check up."

"There are many things on which we could speculate. I want something concrete."

"Naturally."

Singer's gaze had been roving around the room. I saw his glance pass over the floor near the head of the bed, flicker, stop and stare. A moment later he had bent down and picked something up. He held it down near the bedside lamp. I moved over to look at it.

It was a piece of paper torn from an envelope. There was no writing on it, but the postmark was left and a part of the canceled stamp. The date on it was May 26, just two weeks before and the town from which it had been mailed was Preston.

"Evidently she could read," I said.

"Or someone," said Singer. "Someone, somewhere, who once got a letter postmarked Preston."

"All right. Let's not make anything out if it. I haven't noticed us picking up any better clues."

There were voices and footsteps at the front door. Doc and Frank Stauffer came into the bedroom, followed by George Cooler.

Frank Stauffer, Julia's husband, was a steady, upright attorney, whom everybody trusted. He got most of the town's law business. The other lawyer, Jack Sharper, was a lush who had inherited some dough and didn't care whether he got any business or not. Of course, Jack had an unfortunate name for a lawyer.

Frank was tall and stooped and too old-looking for his years. He was about fifty but looked nearer sixty-five. He had thin gray hair that lay smooth against his head, bushy gray eyebrows and a good smile. He was a reserved guy, but friendly with people he respected.

He stepped into the room, looking first at Singer, then at me. He nodded; put his hand on my shoulder and stood looking down at the woman on the bed. George Cooler stood behind Frank, peering over his shoulder. I guess we weren't paying much attention to George because after a minute he moved away and went prowling around the house alone.

Frank Stauffer shook his head.

"That is not Linda Graves," he said. "I would stake my reputation on it. And," he added, with a slight, sly smile, "in a place like Preston, my little reputation is a pretty big thing."

"You don't know who this woman is?" Singer asked.

Frank looked at her again. He shook his head.

"I have no idea."

"You've never seen her before either?"

There was a pause.

"Yes," Frank said, "I've seen her."

Everybody waited. Doc Blane glanced at Frank out of the corner of his eye.

Finally Frank said, "The night before last I came out here. That was the first time anybody saw lights in the house. I'd heard people say Linda Graves was back in town and I wanted to see her. I couldn't understand why she hadn't got in touch with me. It would have been important for her to get in touch with me—important to her.

"I drove out here, thinking surely she'd let me in. But she wouldn't— or this woman, it must have been, wouldn't. She talked to me through the door, but she wouldn't let me in. Her voice was faintly like Linda's as I remembered it, but there was something odd about it, too. When we stopped talking I went back in the bushes, waited a while, then walked around the side of the house. Her bedroom light was on—it was this room—and I looked in. She was doing something to her hair. I got a good look at her face. Then I began to feel foolish, staring into a woman's bedroom, so I went away."

He looked at us.

"That was when I saw her," he said. "I didn't mention it because I didn't want to start a flood of rumors, and she apparently wasn't harming the house. She was an attractive woman—it was just possible that she was a—friend—of some man in town who had put her up here for a few nights."

He stopped. He had made himself clear.

"Are there people in town besides you who have keys to this house?" Singer asked.

"Oh, yes. Jim Dennis has keys. He used to come in to check the plumbing during the winter. Then there's Si Washburn, Seth Graves' old caretaker. Seth had a provision in his will that Si Washburn was to have a place to live the rest of his life. If he had to live in the Graves place, that was all right. And it looks as though old Si's going to live forever."

"That might account for there being a habitable room in the house," Singer said.

"Yes," Frank said. "Si was a good clean old man. Whenever he stayed here he kept the place neat as a pin. Put clean sheets on the bed—all that."

"Where's Si now?" I asked.

"I believe he's visiting his sister up in Traverse City." Singer looked at doc. "You called Sheriff Whitley?"

"Yes," doc said. "He'll be here within an hour."

Singer looked at George Cooler, who had come back into the room.

"You'll want to stay here until the sheriff comes, I suppose," he said.

George's head bobbed up and down.

"Sure," he said.

"We'd better go," said Singer. "Tell the sheriff, George, where we can be found."

George nodded.

"May I ride back with you, Joe?" Frank Stauffer asked. "Doc has to go out north of town and Julia drove our car to Chicago last night."

"Certainly," I said. "Let's go."

As we went out the front door, Frank Stauffer shook his head slowly, sadly.

"I hope the investigation will be discreet," he said. "I hope Linda doesn't get dragged into it."

Doc, Singer and I stared at him. He looked a little embarrassed.

"I think," he said, "we can talk among ourselves without its going further. I've never told anybody. I've been in touch with Linda Graves ever since she went away. I have her letters."

CHAPTER SIX

For twelve hours I almost went crazy.

We just sat around. Nobody did anything. Of course, the thing had got out now and there was plenty of talk. But nothing constructive—just wild gossip.

Then the coroner's inquest concluded that an unidentified woman had come to her death by strangling at the hands of a person or persons unknown. Since nobody knew where she had come from and nobody came forward to claim her, it was arranged to bury her in the cemetery north of town and to set up a simple slab, stating the facts about her as known.

After the inquest, at which both Singer and I appeared and which was held in the showroom of Jake Fisk's funeral parlor on Front Street, we went back to the hotel and were sitting there, not talking much, when Sheriff Whitley came in.

He was a big man, this sheriff. He had to bend down to get through our door and his hands looked as big as watermelons. They were wrinkled and brown like his neck. His eyes were black and sharp. His gray hair was worn thin around the sides of his head. He had a formal, slightly stiff manner, which probably wasn't formal at all when he caught up with and collared the object of his hunt.

He walked across the room and stuck out his hand to Singer.

"Mr. Batts," he said, making a little bow.

"Yes," Singer said.

"I'm Sheriff Whitley."

"I'm happy to know you, sheriff. This is Joe Spinder, my friend and manager of the hotel. Sit down."

Sheriff Whitley walked ponderously over to me and stuck out his hand. I shook part of it. Then he sat down and cleared his throat.

"What beats me," he said, "is that I don't know how to go about identifying that corpse. There weren't any fingerprints in that house. That is, there weren't any that could be used. There were smudges on the doorknob and on the lamp in the bedroom." He looked at me, glaring a little. "You probably did that." I kept still. "But there wasn't a good usable print in the place. We found a pair of gloves in the pocket of her dressing gown. She must have worn them all the time."

"What bothers me," I said, "is that there wasn't any evidence of food around the place. She was there at least three days. Didn't she eat anything?"

"There were evidences of food in her stomach," Sheriff Whitley said. "The autopsy disclosed that she'd eaten something less than four hours before she was killed."

"At what time was she killed, sheriff?" asked Singer.

"Between eleven and twelve o'clock last night, as near as we can determine. However, the food business doesn't mean very much. She could have had a few cans of something, eaten from the cans and then buried them. We haven't searched the grounds. What's on my mind is how we're going to identify her. I've sent pictures all over the country, along with her fingerprints. But there are a lot of people in this country who've never been fingerprinted and the pictures may or may not be much help.

"If she ever got mixed up with the police—and there are a few who don't—they probably won't do any good. Her teeth were all natural, and good. Not a filling, not a false one in her head. There were no marks on her body except an appendectomy scar maybe fifteen years old and a mole in the middle of her back. There was no label in her coat or her gloves."

"Has any check been made on her arrival in Preston?"

"Four nights ago," the sheriff said, "a woman answering her description got off the train at Preston Junction—three miles north of town here. The agent out there saw her, but he was busy and didn't pay any attention. He doesn't know where she came from or where she went. He was going about his business and when he looked up after the train pulled out, she was gone. She hadn't used any of the cars that sit around there earning people back and forth and nobody had picked her up from the road. She just got off the train and walked away. He thinks she was carrying a box or a small bag. He's not sure."

"You're checking the train?" I asked.

"Yeah. The conductor, brakeman and any passengers we can find. Won't be much."

"So," I said, "we've got a book of matches from the 7-11 Club, a piece of envelope postmarked Preston and a note warning me to stay away from Linda Graves."

"That's all," the sheriff said. "And you can pick up matchbooks anywhere—in other towns even—and a postmark doesn't tell us anything except a date. That warning note could have come from anywhere."

"Wait a minute!" I said. "There's something I forgot to tell you. When I came back from the Graves place the other afternoon—yesterday, that is…"

I told them about meeting Julia Stauffer on the country road. As I told it, it seemed to get pretty insignificant. When I got through, I found myself wishing I hadn't brought it up.

"Where's Mrs. Stauffer now?" asked the sheriff.

"Frank told us she went to Chicago," I said. "Must have been on her way there when I gave her a push."

There was a pause. Then Sheriff Whitley leaned forward, he put the tips of his fingers together and he looked straight and steadily at Singer.

This is it, I thought. This is the touch. How will he get out of it this time?

"I figure," Sheriff Whitley said, "we've got to work it this way. We've got to work from the Preston end. We've got to find out why she should have come here and who it is in this town knows about it."

"You think somebody does?" Singer said.

"I'm sure of it."

"Any ideas?" I asked.

The sheriff kept looking at Singer. I didn't count. "That's where you come in," he said.

"I?" said Singer.

"I've heard about you, Mr. Batts. I've heard you have a keen mind for this stuff. I know you've solved a few puzzles—and it hasn't always been appreciated by the authorities. But it has got around. I don't mind saying I'm stumped in this town without some help. I'd like to get that help from you."

Sheriff Whitley was not a guy to hedge around with.

Singer looked at him for a moment, then said, "I'm at your disposal, sheriff. Anything I can do—"

"I know you would. Now the first thing on my mind is this Linda Graves. She lived in that house years ago and everybody thought she was the woman who'd come back. Did you know Linda Graves?"

"Yes. I knew her."

"I hear she went away, sort of disappeared, a long time ago and nobody knew what became of her."

"That is general gossip around town."

"And you don't know anything about what became of her?"

"No, sheriff. I do not."

"The house is still part of the estate and the executor of the estate is Frank Stauffer. Is that right?"

"That's right. Frank's father and Mr. Seth Graves were close friends from boyhood. Frank took over his father's law practice."

"Well, it seems to me that Frank Stauffer would keep a closer check on the place. It seems to me he'd have investigated a little more thoroughly than he did that night he went out there."

"It's logical to think so," Singer said. "I thought so, too, until Frank explained it. He didn't mention this at the inquest, but he was afraid the woman might be the—let's say—paramour of one of our local citizens and he didn't want to embarrass anybody."

"I don't like to embarrass anybody either," Sheriff Whitley said, "but that's an interesting theory. I thought of it myself and I think we'd better check on these local citizens with whom she might have been involved. But—I'd rather you did the checking."

Singer smiled wryly.

"You're asking a lot."

"I know."

"I am well acquainted with practically everybody in this little town and I have a certain stake in not embarrassing any of them."

"But this particular one," the sheriff said quietly, "might be a murderer."

Singer sighed, looked out the window.

"I'll do it," he said, so softly I could hardly hear.

"Fine. Now I'm going to give you an absolutely free hand—but I'm not going to deputize you. I think you'll get along better as a private citizen. I'll back you up in anything you do. I want you to keep in touch with me, of course."

"Of course."

"I've got to get back to Montpelier right now. I'll come back, or call, this evening."

Singer nodded. Sheriff Whitley stood up. He got a firm grip on his hat, stepped over, bowed a little and shook hands with Singer again. Then he came over and did the same with me.

"Thank you," he said, "and good luck."

"I hope I can help you," Singer said.

Without wasting any steps, Sheriff Whitley went out the door.

I looked at Singer.

"A man who comes right to the point," I said. "A little stiff, but practical."

"Very practical. Very demanding."

"So—he's a cop. And right at the moment, now I stop and think about it—so are you."

"Come along, Joe."

"We going to start embarrassing everybody now?"

"Not yet. I want to see Frank Stauffer."

"Oh, yeah. Those letters from Linda."

"Those letters from Linda are more likely than anything else I can think of to give us a clue to the dead woman's identity."

"Frank might not be happy to show those letters around."

"I think he'd rather show them to me than to the sheriff."

"I guess so."

We went out and walked up the street to Frank's office, on the second floor over Thompson's bakery. It was a nice place. I always thought I'd like an office over a bakery. There was a smell of bread baking and those fruit bars Mrs. Thompson specialized in. Best smells in the world, and Frank's office was full of them.

Frank was sitting in his big black leather chair, staring out the window. He swung around when we walked in and stared at us as if wondering who we were. Then he smiled and motioned to a couple of chairs.

"Cigar?" he asked.

Singer shook his head. I took one.

"Ah—" Singer said, "I don't like this a bit. It's going to resemble blackmail. But I promised. I just talked to Sheriff Whitley. He wants to pry into things pretty carefully, and he wants me to pry into the Graves estate. That means you. I noted at the inquest that you said nothing about the letters you told us you'd had from Linda Graves. That's natural enough, since nobody asked you about them. But it occurred to me that perhaps those letters would give us a clue to the identity of this poor woman who has been murdered. I thought you would rather tell me about it than have to drag it all out for the sheriff."

Frank stared at Singer. Then he chuckled.

"Singer," he said, "that's the most intricate apology I ever heard you make."

Singer smiled.

"I'll show you the letters," Frank said abruptly, getting up. "I read them over myself about ten minutes ago. There's no help in them that I can see. But you might find something. You've got a mind like a suction cup."

He went over to a big safe that stood in one corner of the office. He twisted the dial casually, the door opened. He reached in and pulled out a black metal strong box, took a key from his pocket and opened the box. He took some letters out and brought them to Singer. Singer took them. He acted as if he didn't really want to take them, as if he were afraid some old dream would maybe shatter if he read them. I thought maybe he had secretly enjoyed the mystery of Linda Graves.

"They're in chronological order," Frank said. "The first one I had from her is on top. It's twenty years old."

Singer opened an envelope and took out a letter. He handled it carefully, tenderly. It was on cheap, rough typewriter paper and it was typewritten.

"Go ahead," Frank said. "Read it out loud."

Singer read, in his soft, careful voice:

Frank dearest:

I have gone away. By this time you will have guessed it. I wrote a note to daddy and told him about it. When he comes home, you must soften the blow for him. I didn't tell him why, really.

You know why, darling, don't you? Julia trapped you. I know that now. But it's done, and we couldn't go on without hiding from her and I can't stand sneaking out behind the barn. I love you. I'll always love you. I will never return to Preston. Please don't try to find me. I'll write you now and then, but I plan to travel. The postmarks won't help.

You must try to forget me, as I will try to forget you. Please take good care of daddy. I love you.

LINDA.

There was a silence. I looked at the floor. Then Singer said, "I'm sorry, Frank."

"It's all right," Frank said. "The old scars are faint. Read the rest of them."

Singer took the letters one by one and read them rapidly. I stood in back of him and read over his shoulder. There were thirty-five or forty letters, from all over the country—Florida, California, Maine, and a good many from Chicago. Sometimes they would mention friends, but never anybody who came close to answering the description of the dead woman. At one time in her life, Linda had been on the point of marrying someone. She wrote two or three times about him. Then she told how she had found she didn't really love the man, she was unwilling to go through with it and was leaving the country. She would go to Europe for a while. There was a letter after that postmarked Paris.

Many of the letters were brief and were written to acknowledge receipt of money sent by Frank from her father's estate. She had said she wanted Frank to use his own judgment, that she wouldn't interfere.

The last letter had been written only two weeks before. It was from Chicago and it had a slightly different tone from the earlier letters. It was a little sharp. It stated that she had called at the post office every day for a week, expecting a check from Frank, that it had not arrived, that she needed it badly and didn't understand why it hadn't come. She said she planned to leave Chicago in a few days, but would have to wait for the money.

Singer put the last letter back in the envelope and put the packet on Frank's desk.

"Did you send her the check?" Singer asked.

There was a pause. Frank looked out the window. Then he turned back to Singer.

"I sent her a check," he said, "a personal one."

He paused again.

"The truth is, Singer," he said, "Seth Graves' estate is used up. There is no more money—except for one little item, which Linda herself will have to come here to recover."

"What is that?" Singer asked.

Frank hesitated. Finally he said, "I can't tell you. I was sworn to secrecy. And for very good reasons."

"Very well," Singer said. "I'm wondering whether you've engaged in any speculations about this case. Do you have any suggestions?"

"I wish I had. I haven't. There has to be a reason for a woman to come out to a little place like this from Chicago and put up in an old, run-down house. If you can find a reason, you've solved the case. I haven't found one. I searched the papers on the estate—everything I've got. There's nothing."

Frank's telephone rang and he picked it up.

"Hello," he said. "Yes, Jake… Singer is here. I'll ask him… We'll try to get in touch with him right away."

He hung up.

"Do you know where Sheriff Whitley is now?" he asked.

"En route to Montpelier, I think," Singer said.

"We'd better try to get in touch with him. That was Jake Fisk. He says Jim Dennis has been hanging around, annoying him, trying to get a look at the body of that woman."

"Jim must be drunk," I said.

"In a way," Singer said, "yes. He's drunk."

Frank was staring at Singer.

"Twenty-five years ago," he said in a low, dull voice, "Jim Dennis was in love with Linda Graves."

"That is the legend," Singer said.

We went out and downstairs to the street.

* * * *

Jake Fisk's funeral parlor was across the street from Frank's office and a few doors east. We went over there, Singer walking unusually fast. Jake met him at the front door.

Jake was pretty upset. His calm, slightly unctuous manner was gone. He kept running his fingers through his long hair.

"I don't know what's got into Jim," he said. "Been hanging around, trying to get into my—ah—preparation room. Says he's got an idea about the murder, but he's got to look at the corpse. He seems to be pretty drunk."

Jake led the way through his showroom—about as pleasant a place as the inside of a mausoleum—to a sort of little vestibule between the showroom and the preparation room. There was a small table there, a couple of straight chairs and a telephone.

Jim Dennis was sitting on one of the chairs. He was bleary-eyed and his head weaved a little from side to side. His eyes stared dully at the white plaster wall of the little room. He needed a shave badly. The wiry black hairs stuck out from his chin and neck.

Singer put his hand on Jim's shoulder.

"What is it?" he asked.

Jim looked up. His eyes blinked as he tried to focus on Singer's face.

"Who're you?" he said, mumbling.

"What was it you wanted to check on, Jim?"

Jim blinked again.

"Got to find out—" he said. "Got to find out whether she's got a scar on her leg—that time the horse threw her, down by the creek. Got a scar—"

"You're talking about Linda Graves?" Singer said.

A belligerent look came over Jim's face. He lurched up to his feet. I stepped in close beside him.

"Cert'nly," he said. "Cert'nly I mean Linda Graves."

"Jim," Singer said sharply. "The woman who was killed was not Linda Graves."

Jim pushed past Singer and made for the locked door of the preparation room. Jake Fisk, who had been standing around looking worried, went to him and tried to lead him away. Jim swung around and took a poke at Jake. It went wild, but Jake looked more worried than ever.

I got a firm grip on Jim's arm, twisting it just enough to keep him tight against me, pivoted and got him headed into the showroom.

"It isn't Linda Graves," I said. "Let's get out of here now and let Jake go on with his work."

For a few steps Jim went along with me all right. Then, in the middle of the showroom, he jerked away.

"Goddamn it!" he said. "Leave me alone."

I looked at his face. He was crying.

"Take him home, Joe," Singer said.

I took hold of Jim's arm again.

"Let's go home," I said.

"Go home," Jim echoed.

The street door flew open and Esmerelda Granger stood there. She gazed at us. Finally her gaze came to rest on Jim Dennis. She stuck out an arm dramatically, pointed at him, and said in a high, shrill voice,

"*He* was out at the Graves place last night. The night of the—murder."

CHAPTER SEVEN

Jim Dennis stared at her stupidly and finally Esmerelda caught on.

"He's drunk!" she accused, loudly.

"Please—" Jake Fisk pleaded, wringing his hands.

Esmerelda's voice was so piercing that she had attracted some attention and a couple of passers-by had stopped and were peering in over her shoulder. Esmerelda, her eyes fixed on Jim's face, walked forward slowly till she stood very close to us. The curious people from outside pushed through the door and hung around to see what was up.

Singer looked slightly frantic.

"Mrs. Granger," he said, "you claim to have seen Mr. Dennis at the Graves place last night?"

"I did."

Singer frowned.

"But I don't understand. Were you out there last night, too?"

Somebody near the door snickered. Esmerelda stood there and her mouth was open, but she wasn't making any talk.

Singer repeated his question and she still didn't answer. Suddenly Jim Dennis, who had begun to sober up a little, said, "What the hell were you doing out there?"

Esmerelda fidgeted like a wet hen.

"Well—" she said, "it was a perfectly legitimate errand. I was driving by and I saw a light and I thought I would stop and try to talk to Linda—or to the woman—" Esmerelda shuddered a little "—whoever she is—or was."

"What time was this, Mrs. Granger?" asked Singer.

"It was about—well, it wasn't late. It must have been about nine-thirty."

"So you went up and knocked on the door?"

"Well, no. I went around the side of the house. The light was coming from the bedroom and I thought that if I just went back and tapped on the window, I could get her attention."

"And did you?"

"I never got around to it," Esmerelda said. "I went back toward the window and when I got close to it, I saw that somebody was ahead of me, somebody was peering in at her window. I was frightened at first. Then I stopped and thought about it and thought I'd better see who it was. After all—" she hesitated.

"Yes?" Singer said patiently.

"So I went as close as I dared, and saw that it was a man, and when he turned his head a little and the light from the bedroom struck his face, I saw it was Jim Dennis."

"You're absolutely certain of that, Mrs. Granger?" Esmerelda's jaws clamped shut and she nodded vigorously.

"Absolutely," she said, glaring at Jim Dennis.

Singer looked at Jim's face.

"Mrs. Granger says she saw you out at the Graves place," he said.

After what seemed a very long time, Jim said, "Sure, I was out there. What about it? I didn't kill her. I don't even know who she was."

"You were just curious—like Mrs. Granger?"

"Now, you look here, Singer Batts," Esmerelda said. "I won't stand here—"

Singer ignored her.

"Is that right, Jim?"

Jim looked like a whipped puppy. I guess he was whipped, all right, in more ways than one.

"Yeah," he said. "That's right."

"And after you had satisfied your curiosity, you left?"

Jim nodded.

There was quite a little gathering around the door now. I noticed some-body pushing through it. It was Jim Dennis' wife, Alice.

Alice Dennis was a big, stolid woman, with a bitter expression around her mouth. She was as far from Mrs. Granger's type as it was possible to be. She worked hard, minded her own business and rarely mixed in any social doings in town. She had been born and raised on a farm cast of town in a family of eight children, of whom she had been the oldest. She had never known anything except hard work, first on the farm and then with Jim Den-nis. She stood in front of the store now, staring at Jim.

"All right, Jim," Singer said, "you'd better run along home now."

Jim seemed not to hear. There was an absolute hush in the room while I counted silently to ten.

Then Mrs. Dennis said quietly, "Come on, Jim."

Jim heard her. She watched him walk unsteadily across the showroom floor and I found myself wondering how many wives in Preston were haunted by their men's memories of Linda Graves.

Alice Dennis took Jim's hand when he reached her and led him through the crowd, out to the street.

Esmerelda, who had been standing there with her mouth hanging open, came to life.

"Are you going to let him walk away like that?" she asked Singer.

"Why not, Mrs. Granger?" asked Singer.

"But—I saw him out there. He's a suspect. It's not safe—"

Singer closed his eyes, opened them again and tried to look kindly at Esmerelda.

"I can't see," he said slowly, "that I have any more right to suspect him than I have to suspect you."

She gasped.

"I never—" she said.

Jake Fisk could stand it no longer. He stood in the center of his showroom, ran his fingers through his long hair, and said to everybody in general, "Please, will you stop using my showroom for a court?"

Singer looked at the people near the door and said, "Jake is quite right. Let's leave him in peace." Esmerelda stubbornly held her ground.

"I'm not going to stand here under a cloud," she said. Singer looked at her.

"Then may I suggest," Singer said to her, "that you remove yourself into the sunlight?"

She moved herself.

The crowd drifted away then, some of the people following Esmerelda, some going back in the direction from which they originally came. Jake Fisk closed his door, locked it and presumably was at peace again. Singer and I walked down Front Street toward the hotel.

As we crossed the lobby, Harry Baird beckoned to me. I went over to the desk.

"There's a dame in the suite," he said, "wants to see Singer. Says he asked her to come. Looks a little goofy to me. Wouldn't give a name."

"Okay," I said. "Anything else?"

Harry leaned across the desk and whispered.

"Guy sittin' over in the corner, registered a while ago, when you were out. Registered, went up to his room and dropped his bag and come down here and set. Been settin' ever since."

"Waiting for dinner probably."

"Maybe," said Harry. "Don't like his looks."

Singer had gone on into the suite. I followed, glancing into the corner as I went by. The guy sitting there was small and dark. He wore a black suit, a gray felt hat and brown shoes. To me he looked like an ordinary businessman. He was looking straight ahead, paying no attention to anybody.

That was probably why Harry Baird didn't like him. Harry liked people who hung around the desk, made smart cracks and passed the time of day.

Inside the suite, Singer was standing in the middle of the sitting room. Sitting in his own chair, the rocker by the window, was a girl with thick glasses, a loud, flower print dress and-a pink hat. She was talking.

"But Singer, darlin', you practically asked me to come. You wrote this letter—I've got it right here in my pocket—and you said you were anxious to meet me an' could I come for a few days. And I could and did and so here I am. Is there somethin' wrong, honey? I wrote you a letter, tellin' you I was comin'…"

I looked at Singer.

"A special delivery letter?" I asked.

"That's right," she said.

I couldn't stand it to look at Singer. He looked too awful, too beaten. His neck began to redden.

The girl with the glasses looked at me.

"An' this must be Joe Spinder," she said. "I'm mighty pleased to meet you-all. Singer has written so much about you."

"Thank you. I'm afraid I didn't catch your name, miss."

"Bonnie. Bonnie Cavanaugh. I'm from Georgia—originally." She giggled. "Maybe you-all could tell."

I figured it had been a long time since she'd seen Georgia.

Singer finally got something out.

"I'm afraid," he said, "there's been some misunderstanding."

"Oh, no," I said. "Miss Cavanaugh has your letter. You asked her to come down."

"That's right, Mr. Spinder. You see, Singer, you wrote this letter, an'— well, I hope I'm not puttin' you out or anything—"

"You show Singer the letter, ma'am," I said. "He's kind of forgetful. Maybe his mind just sort of mislaid the memory of it. If you show it to him, I'm sure he'll get straightened out."

"Oh, but I'm sure Singer remembers the letters he writes to me. Don't you, honey? I don't want to embarrass him."

"Ahh!" I said. "He won't be embarrassed. Just show him the letter. Singer has been awfully busy. He's a little absent-minded and he needs a little help. Let him see the letter."

She pouted.

"I don't think it's very nice for a gal to come all this way—"

"From Georgia?" I asked.

"From Toledo—"

Toledo was forty miles away.

"For a gal to come all this way and then have to show her boyfriend a letter to prove he asked her to come."

"Her boy-friend?"

"Why, certainly. Singer an' I have been correspondin' for a long time now."

"I don't recall it," Singer said suddenly.

"Through the agency, of course," she said hastily.

Singer cleared his throat.

"I feel that I have been taken advantage of," he said.

"Now, let's not have any quarrels—kids," I said. "If you don't want to show Singer the letter, show it to me. I'll be referee. I'll read it and I'll say, 'Singer, that's what you wrote.' He'll take my word for it."

I stepped over toward the chair. The girl clutched her purse. There were little blue sparks coming out of her eyes now and they were all for me.

"Let's see the letter," I said.

"No," she said.

"Just one little peek," I said. "We'll straighten this all out and then the two of you can kiss and make up."

That got Singer—as I had hoped it would. He looked at me for a moment, horrified. Then he ran from the room. His bedroom door slammed behind him.

I didn't know how deep Singer had got in this, so I took it easy. I sat down at my desk and tried smiling at Bonnie Cavanaugh. I reached into the desk and pulled out a bottle and a couple of glasses.

"How about a shot?" I asked.

She wouldn't look at me. I poured one for myself.

"Look," I said. "It may be that Singer wrote you a letter that gave you the idea you could get away with busting in here. That's all right and that's the way it goes. But I'd better warn you. Singer right now is not himself. He's working on a murder case and he is not thinking about anything else. He can't think about anything else."

She showed a little interest.

"A murder case?"

"Yeah. Singer's a detective, in a way. A private detective. When he gets on a case like this, he's not friendly, and he's not responsible for what he does or says unless it's got something to do with the crime. This particular case involves a woman whom nobody knows. We think it was a woman who did the job. If Singer should get suspicious of you, for instance—"

"Of me? I didn't kill anybody."

The accent had disappeared.

"I don't say you did. I'm sure you didn't. But Singer's concentrating on this case, like I said, and if he should get to thinking about you and the case at the same time—bingo! He'd have you down as a suspect right away. I know. I've seen him work."

"My God," she said, looking straight at me for the first time. "I can't fool around with murder, mister. I'm strictly legitimate. I've been writing to him through this lonely hearts agency and he wrote this letter and a—I—"

"Sure, sure," I said. "It was a good idea. You just picked the wrong time to be a stranger in Preston."

"I guess so."

"Now there's a bus leaving for Toledo in about fifteen minutes. It'll get you back there by 7:30. You wait till Singer finishes this case and then write him a note. I'm sure things will be different then."

"How will I know when the case is finished?"

"You'll read about it in the papers."

"Is he a real detective? Honest to God?"

"Honest to God."

"He never said anything about it in the letters."

"He's modest. Probably told you he was a scholar, studied Shakespeare all the time, and stuff like that."

"He did."

"Don't let him kid you. The only stuff he studies is crime. He's got a library of the bloodiest, goriest books on crime you ever saw. If you ever got tangled up with him, he'd make you read them."

"He doesn't seem like that kind of a guy."

"His appearance will fool you. I've lived with him a long time. I know what I'm talking about."

She got up. "Well," she sighed "I guess I'd better go back to Toledo."

"I guess that would be the best idea. I'd offer to put you up here, but we don't have a single vacancy. And you couldn't very well stay in the suite with us."

She looked me in the eye.

"I could," she said, "but I don't think I will, if you don't mind."

"It hurts my feelings," I said, "but I won't twist your arm."

"So-long," she said.

"Is this your bag?"

"Yeah."

"I'll carry it out for you. Bus stops right out here beside the hotel. Should be along any minute now."

"Should I say good-by to him?"

"Better not," I said. "He's concentrating now. I wouldn't let him get a look at me for a while yet."

I picked up her bag, held the door. We went out. I closed the door of the suite, led the way across the lobby and out the side door. The bus pulled up just as we stepped out the door. I lifted up her bag and the driver swung it to the rack over the seat. Just before she climbed in I gave her a friendly pat on the arm.

"Listen," I said confidentially, "Singer probably told you he had an independent income, small but regular and a good hotel business."

"Well?"

"He doesn't know it yet, but it's about gone. I've padded out the figures, so he wouldn't get discouraged. Truth is, his investments petered out and he doesn't have much of anything regularly. The hotel business in a little town like this is none too good. It's only fair for me to tell you the facts. Singer doesn't know any different yet. But I'll have to tell him pretty soon."

"Thanks for the tip," she said.

"Take it easy," I said.

I stood around till the bus pulled away. It wouldn't stop again till it hit Bridgeville, seven miles down the road. So I knew she wouldn't be getting off and coming back. I thought I'd lied to her so well that she wouldn't ever come back.

I went back up the steps and into the hotel. The stranger in the brown shoes, who had been sitting over in the corner, was leaning on the desk, talking to Harry Baird. When I came in, Harry motioned to me. I went over.

"Mr. Gantner would like to speak to you," Harry said, using his best manners.

He was feeling better now that the guy had broken down and started talking.

"Yeah?" I said. "My name's Joe Spinder."

"Lloyd Gantner," the guy said, holding out a card.

I stuck the card in my pocket and kept looking at him. His eyes were calm, but smoky and they kept changing their size. It fascinated me.

"I'm from Chicago," he said. "There's a place out here for sale and I might be interested in buying it. I was just inquiring about how to find it."

"What place?"

"Known as the 'Graves place,'" he said, his eyes steady now.

"It's at the north edge of town, on the county road. I don't think you can see it right now."

"No? That's too bad. I made the trip on that account. What's the matter?"

"Had a little trouble up there last night. I think the sheriff still has a guard posted."

"Oh, that murder? I read about it in the papers. The place rather caught my fancy."

"I didn't know it was for sale," I said.

"Oh, yes. Man here by the name of Stauffer handles it. Frank Stauffer."

"Frank's office is right down the street."

"I wanted to look the place over first—before I talked to him."

"Well," I said, "you could try it. They might let you look around."

"Thanks," he said. "I'm registered here tonight. I may run out and take a look." He laughed softly. "If I'm not back till late, you'll know the sheriff caught me. Where's a good place to eat?"

"We're serving dinner in ten minutes," I said. "Jack Ruckert's restaurant across the street is also good."

"Thanks," he said and walked away, strutting a little. He went out the main door to Front Street and I saw him standing there, looking across at Jack's restaurant.

Harry Baird said, "Since when is the Graves place for sale?"

"You got me," I said. "Did that guy sound phony?"

"What did you think?"

"I was thinking about something else," I said, looking at him hard.

After a pause, Harry said, "It ain't interesting enough for me to want to mention it."

"Remember that," I said and went into the suite.

Singer was sitting in his rocker. He looked like a hound dog that's been licked for stealing food from the table. He looked miserable. I was sorry for him, but I pulled myself together.

"You see what I mean?" I said. "If you keep fooling around with this matrimonial-lonely-hearts-club business, you're going to get in real trouble. Some dame like that is going to come around and not leave, and there won't be any way out of it. You'll have to marry her."

"I admit I used bad judgment, Joseph. However, it still seems to me that it's a legitimate way to find a congenial mate—"

"No!"

"But how then?"

"I've told you and told you. You go around with a girl and find out whether you get along with her and if you do, some day you ask her to marry you and if she does, it's all over with. Yes, brother! If she doesn't— well, you're just as well off—only maybe at the time you don't realize it."

He shuddered.

"But the direct contact—"

"What the hell do you think this girl had in mind tonight? That, brother, was direct contact."

"I didn't ask her to come. I had no idea—"

"I don't doubt that."

"How did you get rid of her?"

"I told her you were a detective, that you had a criminal mind and that you had absolutely no money."

"Joseph."

"She's gone. No more trouble. She won't be back."

"But—"

"Was it worth it?"

"I guess so."

"Let's go see what Dora's got for us to eat."

"I'm not a bit hungry, Joe."

"You'll be hungry before the night's over, I bet."

"What makes you say that?"

"Come in the dining room. We can talk in there."

He followed me, not because he was hungry, but because he was curious. We sat down at our own table in the far corner and Dora brought in our dinner.

I told Singer about my conversation with the guy in the lobby. He thought it over.

"Strange," he said. "I wonder whether he plans to call on Frank Stauffer."

"I doubt it. I don't think he has any idea of calling on Frank Stauffer— or anybody else."

"Please get Sheriff Whitley on the phone."

I got up.

"What was this man's name?" Singer asked. "Where is he from?"

"Lloyd Gantner. He gave me a card."

I realized suddenly that I had never looked at the card. I pulled it out of my pocket and laid it on the table in front of Singer. It read:

LLOYD GANTNER
7-11 Club
Chicago

CHAPTER EIGHT

I got Sheriff Whitley on the phone and told him the story. He instructed me to keep the guy in sight and he'd come over to Preston as soon as he could make it.

I went back and told Singer what the sheriff had said and that I would find Gantner and keep an eye on him. Singer went into the suite and I went out to the street. In front of the hotel was a big Packard with an Illinois license. I couldn't think of anyone else in town who was visiting from Chicago, so this must belong to Gantner.

I crossed the street and glanced into Ruckert's. Gantner was sitting at the counter eating a steak. I walked on up the street, crossed back, noticed that a light was burning in Jake Fisk's place—poor guy probably having to work all night with that corpse, after the interruption—strolled back to the hotel and went into the lobby. Standing at the desk, I could see the Packard through the front window.

In about ten minutes Gantner came out of the restaurant, strolled slowly across the street and got into his car. My own was parked a few feet away. He sat there for a while, then he tossed a toothpick out the window, started his motor and backed slowly into the street.

I went to the door, stepped out and watched him swing left at the corner and go north. I got in my own car, backed out, waited a minute and went after him.

The sun had just gone down and it was easy to follow him. He was taking his time, rolling along slowly toward the edge of town. At Roy Parker's lumber yard, near the D. T. & I tracks, he slowed so much that I came to a full stop. He bumped across the tracks, shifted into low and went up the grade slowly. Then he straightened out on the county road and went a little faster.

When he stopped near the gate of the Graves place, I stopped about fifty yards behind him and stayed in my car. I saw him get out and walk up to the gate, where one of Sheriff Whitley's deputies was posted. Gantner talked a little and the deputy talked some, too, shaking his head, and then Gantner shrugged and went back and got into his car. He turned it around and headed toward town.

I turned into the middle of the road and set my brakes. He would have to stop. The county road is narrow, with deep ditches on both sides.

He drove to within half an inch of the side of my car and stopped. He got out of the car slowly, leaving his motor running. I got out, too. He was chewing another toothpick.

It was dusk now. There was a soft spring breeze moving in the bushes alongside the narrow country road.

Gantner walked up to where I stood on the right side of my car and smiled. He had a thin, mean little smile.

"Having a little trouble?" he asked.

"I'm all right," I said. "The sheriff would like to talk to you, Mr. Gantner. He'll be at the hotel by the time we get back there."

"The sheriff?"

"Sheriff Whitley."

"Don't recognize the name."

"He's a great guy. You'll like him right away."

"I'm sure of it," Gantner said, still smiling. "I've got nothing against him, and I've got nothing to hide. But I don't feel like talking to the sheriff and I don't like young punks like you following me and talking rough."

I should have been ready for it. It was the tone of his voice that threw me off, I guess. It was hypnotic. Anyway, he brought one up from somewhere near the ground and laid it across my chin and I passed out—right there on the county' road.

I woke up to find the sheriff's deputy squatting beside me, slapping my arms and face. I heard a car coming from a long way off and the deputy grabbed me under the arms and tried to drag me off the road.

I came to enough to help and sat up straight on the edge of the ditch. My head buzzed and my ears ached. There was a bump on the back of my head where it had hit the asphalt of the county road. The sheriff's deputy knelt beside me.

I looked around and saw my car sitting in the ditch, the headlights pointing straight up. It would take a team of horses to get it back on the road. But it didn't look damaged.

"The bastard cold-conked me," I said.

"Yeah," said the deputy, a guy named Hal Smithy. "I got his license number when he stopped to look at the Graves place."

"You got his license number?"

"Sure did."

"That's fine. I know who he is, all right. He's not trying to hide from anybody. He just doesn't care for me personally."

"Oh."

"Where did he go after he got rid of me?"

"Don't know. Lit out like a streak down the road toward town."

"Went fast, eh?"

"Fast as you can go with a big Packard like that."

"That's fast, all right."

"Pretty fast, all right."

"I can't stand any more of this," I said. "Help me up, will you?"

"You all right now?"

"Sure, I'm all right. But it's going to be a long walk into town."

"Only four, five blocks, ain't it?"

"That's right."

"My relief shows up in about ten minutes. If you want to wait, I'll run you in."

"In ten minutes I can be there."

"Guess that's right."

"That's right, all right, all right. The hell with it. You keep a good watch on the Graves place."

"Oh, sure."

"Good-by now. If Morton Seal comes along here with his team, ask him to haul this crate out of the ditch, will you?"

"Don't think I know Morton Seal."

"Neither do I. There ain't any Morton Seal. But a guy might come along with a team and if so, please ask him to haul this crate out of the ditch."

"You sure you're all right, mister?"

"No. But maybe the walk back to town will clear me up."

"Sure. Best thing in the world for a bad knock."

"I thought you'd say that. Good-by."

"So-long. Take it easy."

Walking back to the hotel I thought about this Gantner. In addition to being suspicious of him I was now sore at him. And it didn't help any to have to keep thinking: I don't know anything about him. I've got no reason to suspect him of anything except socking me. That's no crime—not much of a crime. So why did I follow him anyway?

But the question that was in the back of my mind that I kept trying to concentrate on and couldn't was, Is the Graves place really up for sale? And how would a guy like this happen to know about it? And the woman who got killed—did she come to buy the house, too?

Frank Stauffer would know whether the house was for sale, but he didn't know who the dead woman was.

I wondered where Gantner was now. If I found him sitting there at the hotel when I got back, it would go hard with him. It certainly would. But I had a feeling he wouldn't be there.

He wasn't.

Singer was there, and Sheriff Whitley, and a deputy and Frank Stauffer. But not Lloyd Gantner.

I walked into the suite, went to the desk, pulled out my bottle and poured a drink. I didn't speak to anybody. Nobody said anything to me. I drank, set the glass down and looked at the sheriff.

"Little pal didn't want to come," I said.

"Did he go out to the Graves place?" asked the sheriff.

"He did."

I told them about it, all of it, including the humiliating part, with me sitting on the edge of the ditch, listening to the dumb deputy.

"We've got to question him," Sheriff Whitley said. "Mr. Stauffer tells us that so far as he knows there has never been even a rumor that the Graves place was for sale."

"That right, Frank?" I asked.

Frank nodded. He seemed to be trying to make up his mind to tell us something. Finally he did.

"I can think of only one way this might have developed," he said, "and I hate having to tell you, but I guess I'll have to.

"My wife—Julia—has for some time been going on periodic gambling sprees to Chicago. The name Gantner is familiar to me in connection with this. Julia, unfortunately, docs not always win. If she were in debt to Gantner, which is quite possible, if I have him placed correctly, she might have tried to get him to accept the Graves place as security for a large loan. In that case, he would naturally cover up, if he came here to look the place over. I do have a technical right to dispose of the property, if it should be necessary to liquidate the estate. While I couldn't take the money for myself, I could probably arrange an explanation that would satisfy Linda, if she ever inquired about it."

"That sounds a little far-fetched to me," the sheriff said.

"I admit that," Frank said. "It's not much of an explanation. But it's an attempt, and the only one I can make right now."

"That might explain Gantner's presence here," Singer said, "but it doesn't get us any closer to an identification of the dead woman and a motive for her murder."

"Mr. Stauffer," Sheriff Whitley said suddenly, "I don't like to have to ask this, but I think I ought to go through the papers on the Graves estate with you. There's something there, something—there must be—to explain why this woman should be there. I know Mr. Batts has gone over the ground pretty thoroughly, but I'd like to satisfy my own mind on it, too. If you don't mind—"

"Not at all," Frank said. "We can go over to the office right now, if you want to."

"I think we'd better," the sheriff said.

He and Frank got up and went to the door. The sheriff hesitated, turned back and looked at Singer. There was a slight twinkle in his eyes and a little smile on his lips.

"How are we coming along, Mr. Batts?" he asked.

Singer smiled back.

"No comment," he said.

"Maybe Mrs. Granger would be willing to give us some more help," the sheriff said.

We all laughed and Frank and the sheriff went out.

"What about the Julia Stauffer angle?" I asked.

"It's logical," Singer said. "It's logical and possible. But I don't see how we can make much use of it till we can question Julia and Mr. Gantner. I have the feeling that it would be futile to question Gantner and heartbreaking to question Julia Stauffer."

* * * *

This is probably as good a place as any to give you some background on something I mentioned before—about how Frank Stauffer looked older than he was, and tired and the reason some people around town gave for it.

The reason was his wife, Julia.

In her youth, Julia Stauffer had been a beautiful girl. She was the daughter of Corny Ridenour, who at one time owned the bank. She and Frank Stauffer grew up together, were in the same class in high school and later went to the same college. Everybody, including Julia, took it for granted that she and Frank would get married after Frank finished law school.

Then somewhere along the line, Linda Graves stepped into the picture. This was common knowledge around town. It wasn't until Singer and I had read Frank's letters from Linda that we realized how intense the affair had been.

Frank started to court Linda during a summer vacation from college. It went along pretty well, except that Linda on the surface didn't show much enthusiasm for Frank and Julia Ridenour developed a steady and everlasting hatred of Linda Graves. I guess none of us will ever know why Linda pretended not to love Frank.

Frank went back to school, graduated with a law degree and came home to go into practice with his father. He went on courting Linda Graves and everybody waited for a definite break between Frank and Julia—while Julia sat around and sulked and didn't go out with anybody at all.

And then suddenly, one day about three months after Frank's graduation, he and Julia announced their engagement and two weeks later they were married. Linda Graves did not go to the wedding.

It was only three months later that Linda disappeared. Her father, Seth Graves, was away in the east, looking after some relatives and when he got back, Linda had been gone for several days. It must have been a shock to Seth to come back and find Linda gone and a lot of people wondered why he didn't investigate, or look for her. But Singer told me that Seth was a patient, kindly man, who saw that Linda could never live happily in Preston. And the old man understood his daughter well enough to accept her leaving, as long as she kept in touch with him, and didn't try to bring her back.

He lived out the last years of his life alone, with the help of Si, the caretaker. In the last two years of his life, he was blind. He died in 1925.

I asked Singer once why Linda hadn't come back to Seth's funeral and Singer said that from reading Frank Stauffer's letters from Linda he had figured out that she was in Europe then. He knew that one of Seth's relatives in the east had wired to Preston and asked to have the body shipped back there for burial. Nobody in Preston had any contacts with the eastern relatives.

Well—after Julia Ridenour had Frank sewed up and married, she settled down to being what the people had always suspected she was—a first-class bitch.

Julia liked to live fast and expensively. Frank only made a moderate amount of money and Julia spent all of it as fast as it came in. She drank hard and talked hard. The neighbors would hear her yelling at Frank when she'd taken a little too much. She liked to ride and she killed three horses in a year—rode them to death. She would go to Chicago every three weeks or so, leaving Frank behind, and spend her time in expensive clubs, gambling away everything Frank had made. Many times he had had to go up there and bring her home.

Why he never got rid of her, nobody ever figured out. People speculated that the reason Julia turned into such a tramp was that although she had captured Frank and got him to marry her, she knew she could never destroy his love for Linda Graves. This made her so angry that she took it out on Frank. That always seemed a little fanciful to me and I figured that Julia was that kind of a woman and would have turned out that way no matter who married her. But I might be wrong.

Anyway, Frank Stauffer was aged before his time and a lot, if not all, of the reason for it was the life he led with Julia.

Singer obviously wanted to be left alone to think things over, so I kept my mouth shut, went over and mixed another drink and sat down to drink it. I was about halfway through it when the phone rang.

It was Jake Fisk. He sounded excited.

"Look, Joe," he said, "can you and Singer come over here right away? I've found something Singer might want to see."

"We'll come right over," I said.

I told Singer about it and he was out of his chair before I'd finished the first sentence.

"Jake's light's in the back!" I said. "We'd better go in that way."

We went down the alley to the "service" entrance to Jake's place. There was a little white light over the door and I knocked. Jake opened up and led us through his garage, past the hearse and ambulance into the back room and through there into his preparation room.

The body was lying on the table in the center of the room and Jake had thrown a sheet over it. That was all right with me. The odor of death and embalming fluid was strong in the room.

Jake was excited all right. He reached into his pocket with trembling fingers and pulled out a small piece of paper. It was soft paper, very old and cracked and torn and ragged around the edges. It had rolled up very tightly into a small cylinder and Jake spread it out and held the edges down so we could see it.

It was a map, rough, crudely drawn, showing a house, trees, a barn, and so on. It was hard to make it out.

"It's a map of the Graves place," Singer said. He looked at Jake. "Where did you find it?"

Jake looked puzzled.

"The autopsy wasn't very thorough, I guess. This was rolled up in a tiny little roll and taped to the little hollow in the back of her head, where her long hair would cover it. I can show you where she'd shaved the short hair off to make a little pocket for it."

Jake reached for the sheet to show us.

"We'll take your word for it," Singer said.

"I called you instead of the sheriff," Jake said, "because I didn't want to get anybody in trouble—you know, because it hadn't been found before. I noticed it a little while ago. My fingers brushed against it as I was arranging her on the table. I got to thinking about Jim Dennis wanting to see the body this afternoon."

"I'm glad you told me," Singer said. "Every shred of evidence of any kind is something we can use."

"Is it a good map?" I asked.

"It's quite good, has considerable detail. It shows the house and the barn, the trees, gives distances. It marks a certain spot with an X and it gives directions for reaching that spot."

"Like playing pirates," I said. "What do you think the X refers to?"

"I don't know."

I was looking at the map.

"It's signed," I said.

"Yes," said Singer.

Down in the right-hand corner, written in pencil, were the words, *"Seth Graves—1925."*

"How do you suppose this woman came to have it?" Jake Fisk asked.

"When we know that," Singer said, "we'll know a good deal. Joe, did the sheriff say something about leaving me to my own devices?"

"Yeah."

Singer thought it over.

"For some very good reasons of my own," he said, "I don't want to tell the sheriff about this yet. I don't want to tell anybody about it."

"Of course," I said, "the sheriff also told you he would want you to keep him informed."

"I have no intention of withholding anything from him indefinitely."

"It's up to you," I said.

There was the sound of a car in the alley. It stopped. Singer folded the map carefully and put it in his pocket.

"We must go have another talk with Jim Dennis," he said.

I heard footsteps outside, in Jake's garage. A moment later there was a knock at the door. Jake glanced at us, stepped over to the door and opened it. I saw him stiffen and then he backed away from the door into the middle of the room.

The door opened wider and two men came in. They both had guns. I had never seen either of them before. They were both big, with padded shoulders and they both wore hats. Their faces were strictly poker.

One of them motioned to Jake to move over closer to Singer and me. Jake did. The guy held the gun steady, looking at us without blinking. The other put his gun away, stepped over to the table and pulled back the sheet from the face of the corpse. He nodded at the other guy, covered the face again. He lifted the body, wrapped the sheet around it carefully, hoisted it to his shoulder and headed for the door.

"Wait a minute!" Jake Fisk said, and the guy with the gun poked it toward him and said, "Shut up."

Then he poked the gun at me.

"You," he said. "Come along."

"Me?"

"Come on."

I looked at Singer.

"Been awfully nice knowing you," I said.

The guy with the gun said, "We got nothing against this joe; we're just taking him along for a little while. Don't come after us."

"This is a pretty serious offense," Jake Fisk said.

"Yeah, bud," the gunman said. "Keep your shirt on. This will just relieve you of a little hard work."

He waved his gun at me and jerked his head. I went along, feeling foolish, because I didn't think he would shoot any of us if I refused, and still, I wasn't quite sure. When you're not quite sure, you always go the way the gun goes.

The guy carrying the corpse went out first. The second guy stepped aside to let me pass and I followed the first one through the garage into the alley. There was a black sedan parked, with the motor running and the doors open. The guy with the corpse climbed into the back seat, set the body down on the seat and sat down beside it. Something nudged me in the back.

"Get in," the gunman said, and I climbed into the back seat and sat down on the other side of the guy who was squiring the body. The guy with the gun slammed the back door and climbed into the driver's seat. He started the car with a lurch and we roared down the alley, turned left toward Front Street, right at Front Street, and by the time we passed the hotel we were making fifty-five easily. When we hit the bridge just west of town, the guy failed to slow down and we dipped, bounced and all of us bumped our heads against the ceiling. The guy beside me said, "Goddamn it!" and took off his hat and straightened it out. The corpse didn't say anything and neither did I. I rubbed my head and thought, "Oh, hell."

We kept on jouncing around all the way down the county road, because the county road is rough and these guys were in a hurry. When we hit the highway—if we ever hit it—it would be smoother. I started to tell them about where the big-bumps were, but nobody paid any attention so I gave up.

The guy beside me reached over and started monkeying with the corpse.

"What's the matter," I asked him, "don't live girls go for you?"

He set the corpse down slowly, turned his head and looked at me. He hadn't said anything in all the time I'd known him except "goddamn it" and his voice came as a shock to me.

"Listen," he said, "I think we got time to stop and work you over—if you don't keep your mouth shut—any way you want it."

"Sorry," I said. "I'll shut up."

"Find anything?" the driver called back.

"We got a smart boy back here," the guy said.

"Dump him," the driver said.

The guy nudged me with his knee.

"Open the door," he said.

"Look—" I said.

He lifted his right leg a little and brought his heel down on my toe. It was a good trick. It hurt like hell and I hollered.

"Open the door."

I reached for the handle of the door.

"The wind will rip it right off the hinges," I said.

"It's reinforced," the guy said. "Open it."

I opened it. The wind tore it out of my hand and it flew all the way open. But it stayed on.

"Get out," the guy said.

That was all right, except that we were going sixty-five miles an hour and I wasn't quite ready. We were nearing the sharp curve in the county road that would bring us into the highway and I knew they would have to slow down more than they expected to. I tried to stall.

I heaved myself up from the seat slowly. Too slowly, I guess. The guy beside me stuck his hand against the small of my back and pushed. Fortunately, at that moment we hit the curve and the brakes screeched as the driver slowed. But we were still making good time.

I jumped when he pushed me and cleared the car. There was a ditch on the curve, full of weeds and I managed to land in them on my hands and knees and then I turned my shoulder under and rolled with the momentum.

The momentum went on till I got to the bottom of the ditch and started up the other side. The jar had been gorgeous and I got up, rubbing my shoulder and then my head and crawled up the side of the ditch to the road on my hands and knees.

The nearest house was George Sikes' place half a mile back toward town. I didn't know whether George had a telephone or not.

It was a cloudy night and the county road was dark as tar. I walked on the right side, hoping somebody would come along and pick me up.

Nobody came along and I got to George Sikes' place and went up and knocked on the door. George's daughter, Genevieve, opened it.

"I'm not a tramp," I said, "I'm Joe Spinder."

I guess I looked more beat up than I had realized. "What happened?" she asked. "You have a wreck?"

"In a way," I said. "Do you have a telephone?"

"Yes," she said, "but it's out of order."

"Fine," I said.

"Don't you have your car? How did you get way out here?"

"It's a long story," I said. "But I don't have my car and I've got to get back to town."

"I'll take you," she said. "Come on in."

I stepped into the Sikes' parlor. Genevieve was wearing jeans and a blue denim shirt. She was a nice-looking girl. I watched her move across the room and thought about how maybe I wasn't in such a hurry after all. The parlor was comfortable, the lamps turned down. I had been out with Genevieve a few times and it had always been fun. Then I thought of the corpse taking a ride with the two mugs and Singer standing around, wondering how soon it would be safe to send after me, and I pulled myself together and gave up the idea of smooching with Genevieve.

She came back into the room with a leather jacket on.

"We'll have to take the pick-up," she said. "Dad and mom went into town with the car."

"Anything," I said. "Anything at all. Sorry to put you out."

"Forget it," she said.

I followed her through the house and out the back door. We went out to the barn and I opened the door. I stepped on a snoozing chicken that put on a mad scene loud enough to wake every animal on the place.

"I hate chickens," I said. "Why don't you sell them?"

"They lay eggs," she said.

She climbed into the seat of the pick-up truck and I followed her.

Genevieve could drive anything. She backed out of the barn and down the road about thirty miles an hour, turned onto the road and got headed toward town in a couple of seconds, without grinding a gear and without jerking once.

"What happened?" she asked.

I told her about the corpse snatching and how the boys dumped me on the curve.

"My God!" she said. "You mean you had to ride down the road with a dead body?"

"The body didn't give me any trouble," I said. "It was the evil companions that upset me."

"You poor boy."

"It's all right now, ma. Don't be sorry."

"Has Singer solved the murder yet?" she asked.

"Not yet. Have you?"

Genevieve wasn't much for talk that small. She ignored me.

"You want to stop at Elbert Adam's place and call?" she asked.

"More fun riding with you," I said. "Let's just get into town."

"Those men will have a big head start."

"The hell with them."

Genevieve let it go. We were burning up the road and the eight miles into town didn't seem like much. When we came to the bridge, she slowed down.

"Let's have a date some night," I said.

She smiled a little, and then she said, "You know where to find me, Joe."

Then I felt like a heel and decided not to talk about it. But I would certainly remember to call her.

She made a U-turn at the corner of Front and Oak Streets and pulled up in front of the hotel.

"Don't you get tired of living in a hotel?" she said.

I looked at her and it was my turn to smile.

"Not yet, darling," I said. "Not yet."

She slapped my face. I kissed her and she kissed me back. "Thanks for the ride," I said. "You're wonderful."

"Good night," she said.

I got out and the pick-up raced away down Front Street. I went into the hotel lobby. Jack Pritchard, the night clerk, was on duty. I would just as soon not have had to say anything to him. His nose always went up in the air with disapproval whenever Singer got launched on an investigation. But Singer's father had said in his will that Jack was to have a job at the hotel as long as he wanted it, and we had to put up with him.

"How's business?" I asked him.

He looked me over and I could see him sniffing mentally. I wasn't neat.

"All right," I said, "I just got thrown out of a gangster's car. So I don't look so nice. Where's Singer?"

"Mr. Batts"—he always called him Mr. Batts—"is out at Jim Dennis' place. He advised the sheriff of your—trouble—and said that you should pick him up at Jim's house. He also wants you to reserve three seats on the midnight train to Chicago."

"Oh, he does? In what will I pick him up? My car is sitting in a damn ditch out north of town."

"Your car is parked out in front of the hotel," Jack said. "It was brought in about half an hour ago."

You snooty, superior bastard, I thought.

"Get Ed Lambert on the phone for me," I said.

Jack didn't like me ordering him around, which is mainly why I did it. Ed Lambert was the agent at the station at Preston Junction.

Jack got him on the line. I took the phone away from him.

"Ed," I said, "three seats on the midnight train to Chicago."

"Sure, Joe," Ed said. "What's up?"

"My dander," I said.

"Pardon?"

"That's quite all right. We'll pick up the tickets."

"Okay."

I was in a lousy mood. I slammed the receiver and handed the phone back to Jack Pritchard.

"Do you suppose Singer would mind if I showered and dressed before I picked him up?" I asked.

"I wouldn't have any idea," Jack said.

"I thought you wouldn't," I said.

I went into the suite. In the bathroom I stood in front of the mirror and looked at myself. I was not very good looking right then. I had a big bruise—red-yellow-blue in color—on one cheekbone and a big smear of dirt across that side of my face. My shirt collar had dug into the ground and got messed up and there were big smudges on my shoulder and on the front of my coat.

"Why is it?" I said to myself, into the mirror, "that I always take such a beating whenever we try to solve a crime?"

It wasn't bitterness that made me feel lousy. It was just that I kept thinking about Genevieve Sikes and wishing that I were where she was now instead of banging around with corpses, gamblers and gunmen.

I took off my clothes, got under the shower and washed off most of the dirt, put on a different suit and went out and found my car. Jack had been right. It was parked right in front of the entrance, the key in it. There was a note on the handle of the door. I took it off and held it up under the street lamp to read it.

Dear pal,

    I couldn't get around to this until after dinner, because I was late getting home and Ginny don't like me to miss my supper. I hope the car is okay.

MORTON SEAL

I looked around to see whether anybody on the street was gazing at me strangely. Nobody was gazing at me at all. I got in the car, put the note in my pocket and drove down Front Street toward Jim Dennis' house.

CHAPTER NINE

I went up on Jim Dennis' front porch and rang the bell. After a minute Alice Dennis opened it.

"I'm looking for Singer," I said.

"He and Jim just left a few minutes ago," she said. "Singer said you were to meet them at the Graves place."

"Oh, thanks," I said and turned and started away.

I had got to the edge of the porch when Alice Dennis' voice came from behind me. It was a quiet, urgent, appealing voice.

"Joe."

I turned back.

"Yeah?"

"Joe—does Singer suspect Jim of murdering that woman?"

"Of course not," I said. "That's silly."

"He didn't do it," Alice said.

"I'm sure he didn't."

"Then why does Singer keep after him this way? He came out here and wanted to know why Jim wanted to see that poor woman's body. He kept asking him about it. Jim couldn't tell him. He was drunk. He just got the idea in his head that the woman was—Linda Graves."

"That's what I thought."

"Listen, Joe. Jim didn't kill her. I know he didn't."

It sounded as if she were arguing about it.

"You have some reason to be so sure?" I asked, trying to sound casual.

There was a pause. Then Alice said, "Yes. I know he didn't. I know because I was out there that night. I followed him."

"I guess the whole town was out there that night."

"He acted so queer that day I got worried. When he went out, about nine o'clock, I followed him in the other car. I saw him drive up the road past the Graves place and park, and walk back, and I followed him up to the house. He looked through the window there, like Esmerelda Granger said, and then he went around back and went in the house. I looked in the window and he was sitting in there, talking to the woman. She was showing him something. After a while he got up and went out the front door. The woman was alive after he left."

"Why didn't you tell Singer that?"

"I was afraid to let Jim know I followed him."

"I don't think you have a thing to worry about at all, Mrs. Dennis," I said. "I'm sure Singer doesn't suspect Jim. You just hang on and wait and this thing will be all cleared up before you know it."

"I hope so. Jim ought not to be hounded that way."

"Well, don't you worry about it."

"You won't tell Jim, will you—what I just told you?"

"Not a word."

"I guess—maybe—you better tell Singer."

"Yeah. I guess maybe I better had."

"That's all," she said. "That's all I know."

"I think you were right to tell me, Mrs. Dennis. Good night."

"Good night," she said.

I went to my car and started for the Graves place. I got to thinking about Genevieve Sikes again and began to feel very blue and sorry for myself. To get away from that, I tried to feel sorry for the woman who had got murdered, but she was too dead. I couldn't work up much feeling for her.

I parked the car on the road near the gate of the Graves place. Jim Dennis' car was sitting just inside the gate on the drive. I walked past it and climbed up to the house.

There were no signs of life inside, no lights. I looked around the corner, toward the back. There was the dull gleam of a flashlight back near the barn. I went back there.

Jim Dennis was holding a flashlight. I followed the beam of it and saw Singer, on his knees, digging around in the dirt with a stick. This looked so silly to me all of a sudden that I laughed. Jim Dennis' head jerked around. When he saw who it was, he looked away again, but he didn't say anything.

Singer said, without looking around, "Hello, Joseph."

He was turning things up with the stick—empty cans they were. They looked new, as if they had been opened recently, emptied and buried. I made out a can of beans, a can of spinach and a can of brown bread.

"She ate a well-balanced diet," I said.

"Speak softly of the dead," said Singer.

"Excuse me."

He seemed to be a little touchy. I guessed he was worried. Usually he was the gentlest guy in the world. But when he got worried about finding something he would get a little sharp, a little hard to handle.

Singer left the little pile of cans where he'd found them and moved on. There was a freshly turned spot of earth about two feet across and he hesitated, looked around, then got down on his knees and prodded some more with the stick. He dug for quite a while. I got down and helped him. The earth was all soft and you could tell it had been stirred up recently. But we found no cans, no scraps. Nothing but dirt.

"Strange," Singer said, under his breath. "Very strange."

He stood up and brushed the dirt off his hands.

"What the hell am I doing out here?" Jim Dennis asked.

Singer looked around.

"Thank you for bringing me out here, Jim. Now that Joe's back, I guess we can manage."

"Well, I'll get on home," Jim said.

He handed me the flashlight, turned and walked away.

Singer took the light, flashed it on me.

"Did they hurt you?" he asked.

"No. They tossed me out at the curve in the county road."

"I'm glad you got back safely and so soon."

"I'm all right. What are we looking for out here?"

"This was a fishing expedition. It failed. I felt—still feel—sure that Jim Dennis knew of the existence of that map. I wanted to get him to say something about it. But he wouldn't. He insisted he was drunk and kept thinking the body was that of Linda Graves."

"Do you think Jim killed her?"

"I don't know."

"I hope not, because I just assured his wife that you didn't."

"Did Alice Dennis tell you something?"

"Yeah."

I told him. He listened carefully and when I got through he nodded his head.

"That helps," he said.

"It don't seem to help me."

"It will, Joseph, it will."

"What's the idea digging around near the barn? I thought that X on the map was out in the middle somewhere."

"That's right."

"Why don't we do a little digging out there?"

"For the very good reason, Joe, that I don't think the time is ripe for it."

"Did you tell Jim about finding the map?"

"No. I've told nobody. I wanted Jim to do the leading." I looked at my watch.

"The time is ripe for us to catch the train to Chicago," I said. "Who's going with us, and why are we going? And what about those guys with the corpse?"

"Sheriff Whitley has notified the Chicago police of the affair and asked them to pick up Gantner and keep a check on burials."

"I don't know whether these boys were going to Chicago or not. Maybe they doubled back. They might have come from anywhere."

"The sheriff has been in touch with police in other cities, too, and with the state officers."

"So why are we going to Chicago?"

"We are going to get Julia Stauffer, to have a talk with Mr. Gantner and to try to find Linda Graves. Frank Stauffer is going with us."

"I don't give a damn about Julia or Gantner," I said, "but I would certainly like to see this Linda Graves."

"And so would I, Joseph."

"Where do we meet Frank Stauffer?"

"At the junction. We'll have to go back to the hotel and get our bags."

"We'd better get the hell about it."

We got in the car. On the way to the hotel I said, "Is there anybody in Preston named Morton Seal?"

"Not that I know of," Singer said.

"I thought not."

"Why do you ask?"

"No reason. Nothing at all. The world is full of clowns."

"I'm sure of it. But I don't catch the conclusion."

"Don't worry about it. I guess we've got enough to think about."

"Exactly. And I would appreciate your not mystifying me any more than is absolutely necessary."

"Very good."

I went into the hotel and got our bags, which Dora had packed for us. I stopped by the desk and glared at Jack Pritchard.

"We're going to Chicago," I said. "We'll be back sometime. Don't dip into the till."

Jack got purple in the face. He was too mad to say anything, which was just fine with me.

I burned up the road to the Junction and we made it five minutes before the train was due. Frank Stauffer was waiting for us. I parked the car, asked Ed Lambert to have somebody drive it back to the hotel sometime and we got aboard.

CHAPTER TEN

The midnight train to Chicago was comfortable and fast. It was a four-hour run. It was the only train on the road that kept a sandwich and bar service running all night. There were no berths available at our point on the line, only parlor seats.

Singer and I had seats side by side and Frank Stauffer was across the aisle and one seat ahead of us. I was sleepy when I got on, but I knew Singer wouldn't sleep, so I ordered a sandwich and a bottle of beer and tried to stay awake.

Singer sat with his eyes closed, his long legs stretched out in front of him. He didn't say anything and I ate my sandwich and drank my beer slowly. When I finished, I rang the bell and the boy came and picked up the empty plate and bottle. I looked at Singer. He might have been asleep, but I knew he wasn't. He never sleeps.

"What's all that stuff with the map?" I asked.

"There have been rumors, Joseph," Singer said, "to the effect that Seth Graves buried some money in his back yard before he died. You've heard the rumors."

"Yeah."

"I never put much stock in them myself. One reason I talked to Jim Dennis tonight was to draw him out on his attitude toward the rumors. Jim's connection with the Graves house has been rather close. He claimed, when I asked him, that he had never believed the rumors cither and that he had never seen any evidences of their substantiation."

"Sounds like a stall, after what Alice told me."

"Exactly. I think we have reason to believe that Jim did put some stock in those rumors. Undoubtedly the paper his wife said the woman showed him was the map."

"How many other people know about the map, I wonder?"

"I am beginning to think that a lot of people know about it, possibly including even Mrs. Esmerelda Granger."

I lowered my voice.

"Do you think it was that idea that Frank was talking about when he said that Linda herself would have to come back to get what remained of the estate?"

"I think it's quite possible. Certainly the map must have been in his possession—or—"

He paused.

"Or—?" I said.

"Or in the possession of Linda Graves, from whom, at some time, it was stolen."

"And that is why we're going to Chicago?"

"That is why."

"Do you think we can find Linda?"

"We have the name of the bank where she cashed the latest check Frank sent her. We have the Chicago police making a check for us. That's about all. I wrote her a short note, general delivery, in the hope she might call for some mail and would pay some attention to my request that she meet us. I don't know. I'm not hopeful, but I think there is a chance—a long, slim chance."

"Now I've got the picture, do you mind if I go to sleep?"

"Not at all."

"Maybe this woman strangled herself," I said, "after she found she wasn't getting any closer to the buried treasure."

"Doubtless, and removed the instrument by which it was accomplished, after she had composed herself in another world."

I looked at him.

"You talk beautiful, you know, when you get going."

"Please don't let your own shortcomings lead you to ridicule what you cannot achieve."

"Okay. Shall I go to sleep now?"

"Please do."

I did. I had a bad dream about Lloyd Gantner and awoke in the cold dawn, swearing, hearing the porter calling, "LaSalle Street—Chi—cago!"

We got off and went out to the cab stand. Frank suggested a medium-sized hotel on the near North Side and we went out there. They had a suite—two adjoining double rooms. Singer and I took one and Frank the other.

We went to bed and I pounded my ear till ten o'clock. I don't know what Frank and Singer did, but Singer was wandering around the room, fully dressed, when I woke up.

* * * *

Singer wasn't very talkative at breakfast and I left him alone. Frank hadn't said a word about getting in touch with Julia and I didn't bring that up, either. It was *his* wife. Frank, as a matter of fact, hadn't said many words about anything at all.

With photographs of the dead woman, we went to police headquarters. It took about half an hour to find the guy who knew what we wanted. His name was Lieutenant McMichaels. He was a good guy.

He leaned back in his swivel chair and asked, "How's Sheriff Whitley? He used to be on the force here. A fine fellow."

"We like him very much," Singer said.

"I'm afraid I don't have much for you," the lieutenant said, picking up a file. "Identification doesn't have a thing on the victim, and nothing on Linda Graves, except that a woman by that name got a parking ticket about ten years ago. Missing Persons has also checked and found nothing."

"What about our stolen corpse?"

The lieutenant shook his head.

"Every mortician in town has been alerted. So far no reports. Of course there are some of them who are not scrupulous and who would bury a body for the right amount of money and ask no questions."

"Did you pick up Gantner?"

"We picked him up late last night. We asked him what he had been doing in your town and he said he had gone to look at a house there—as you reported. We didn't really have enough on him to hold him. He might have been telling the truth. Gantner is a smooth operator. We know he runs a gambling outfit and has his fingers in some other rackets, but we can't get hold of him."

"There is the possibility," Frank said, "that he was involved in the stealing of the murder victim's corpse."

"I thought of that," Lieutenant McMichaels said. "We've had a couple of boys tailing all of Gantner's known henchmen. A couple of them looked fishy, but there's nothing definite on them yet."

"Well—" Singer said, and stood up.

"I'm afraid I'm not much help to you," McMichaels said.

"You have a difficult problem," Singer said. "I don't criticize you in the least. But I think that Joseph and I had better get busy."

We shook hands all around and Lieutenant McMichaels said, "Don't hesitate to call on me for any help you need."

"Thank you," Singer said.

"He was pretty polite," I said as we went out.

"I believe Sheriff Whitley called him about us."

Out in the street, Frank said, "I've got to look up Julia. I may bring her back to the hotel with me. You won't mind?"

"Not a bit," Singer said.

"Then I'll meet you later," Frank said, "and good luck."

"Transportation," Singer said and I hailed a cab.

Singer directed the cabbie to all the newspapers in town, in whatever order was most convenient. At each place we went to the classified ad department and Singer placed in the Personals column an ad that read:

Linda Graves: Imperative you get in touch with Singer Batts at once. Phone Superior 9911, Room 402.

Two of the papers promised that it would get into the late afternoon editions.

It was lunchtime then and Singer allowed me to lead him into a restaurant on Wabash, where I had lunch and he drank a cup of coffee. He looked very worried, but when I tried to get him to talk about it, he evaded my questions and talked about something else.

I finished my second cup of coffee, pushed the plates back, lit a cigarette.

"Look," I said, "when I was a road stiff I spent a lot of time in Chicago. Used to hole up here in the winter. I know a guy who used to hang around with me—one of my best friends. A tough boy, but smart and well acquainted. Knew every petty racketeer, gambler and cop in town. We called him Whitey. If I can find him, maybe we can get a line on Gantner."

"Let us find him," Singer said, getting up.

I paid our check and we left the restaurant and got a cab.

Out on West Madison we got out.

It was the same old place—the flophouses on both sides, the cheap hash joints, the same broken-down stiffs wandering around, soaking up the sun or sitting in the open windows of the fifty-cent hotels.

The good bar was still on the corner. It was big, airy and—unusual for here—clean. It had been here in the old days, too, but then I hadn't patronized it much—only when I had a couple of bucks.

Singer and I went, in and sat down at the bar. I didn't remember the bartender. We ordered beers. There was a big bowl of cheese and a jar of crackers sitting on the bar and I spread a few.

"Best cheese in Chicago," I said. "Better have some."

Singer drank some beer and readied for a cracker.

There was only one other customer in the place and the bartender wasn't busy. He wiped the bar, handed me another beer when I motioned to him and then turned to monkey with a little radio on the back bar. I drank the second beer and asked for a third.

I gave him a bill for the third one, and before he could turn away, I asked, "Ever see Whitey Callahan?"

He gazed over my head, his face impassive, snapped the bill between his fingers, turned and rang it up. He turned back, laid the change on the bar and reached for his bar rag. He wiped the spot where my glass had been.

"Whitey comes in once in a while," he said.

He turned away. I nudged Singer and pointed to his glass, which was still half full. He drank it down and I called for another beer for him.

When the guy set it down, I said, "Would I be wasting my time waiting for him?"

"Couldn't say, mister," the bartender said and it was clear that that was all the information I was going to get out of him.

I decided we might as well wait a while. But I would have to slow down on the beer. I'd drunk four glasses in a hurry and on top of the lunch it was making me a little dopey.

A couple of guys came in and sat down at the bar. I looked at them through the mirror. Neither was Whitey.

Singer looked at me appealingly.

"I cannot drink any more beer," he said.

"Whisky?"

"I don't know—"

I got the bartender.

"Straight shot and a glass of water," I said.

Singer tasted the whisky tentatively. Then he drained the shot glass and asked for another. That made me feel a lot better. When Singer starts taking whisky, he's in a case for fair. He never drinks at any other time.

There were two entrances to the place—one right on the corner, which we had used, and another a little way down the side street, behind where we now sat at the bar. There were some booths along the back wall.

At about the time Singer ordered his third shot, this side door opened and two guys came in. One of them came to the bar, the other went to one of the booths and sat down. The guy at the bar didn't mean a thing to me but there was something familiar about the one who went to the booth.

I couldn't see him in the mirror so I got up and went to the door in the back marked "Men!" which was at one end of the row of booths. I took my time, looking the guy over as I went. I got a good look at him as I went through the door. It was Whitey.

I came back and sat down at the bar. The bartender went down to the other end and I spoke softly to Singer.

"Whitey's in a booth in the back. Let me go first. You come over in about five minutes."

Singer nodded and I got off the stool and carried my beer glass back to the booth. Whitey was studying a racing form. I stood there.

"Hi, Whitey," I said.

His head jerked up. His little black eyes studied me for a long time. Then he broke into a wide grin.

"God Almighty!" he said. "Little Joe!"

"How are you?"

"Sit down, Joe me boy. Sit down."

I sat down. Whitey was still grinning. Then suddenly the grin disappeared and he looked at me seriously, a wrinkled line in his forehead.

"Joe," he said softly, "you legitimate?"

"Always was," I said.

"Yeah, I know, but—"

"Sure," I laughed. "I'm even respectable. Working. Been managing a hotel for five years."

"In Chi?"

"No. Little country town."

He grinned again.

"Me—I'm legitimate for five years now. Gotta be careful."

"I know."

Singer came over to the booth. Whitey's face turned suspicious again.

"Whitey," I said, "this is Singer Batts, owns the hotel I manage."

Whitey looked him over from head to toe. I guess he decided there couldn't be anything to worry about from a guy like Singer, because the grin came back again and Whitey's head bobbed.

Singer sat down and I looked at Whitey.

He was a bristly-black-haired Irishman, built like a tackling dummy— all head, shoulders and chest. What teeth hadn't been knocked out of him were bad. But he was a clean guy. I'd bunked with him from time to time. He had big hands, with thick veins standing out on them and these sharp, shrewd little black eyes. He was a tough guy, Whitey, but a happy one.

"Singer and I are looking for a couple of people," I said. "I thought maybe you could help."

"Maybe," Whitey said.

A girl came with lunch for Whitey. She set it down on the table. It consisted of six tamales, a bowl of chili and a huge pile of white bread. Whitey picked up a slice of bread, rolled it up and dunked it in the chili.

Singer was carrying a large envelope with the photos in it. I slid it out from under his arm, found a pretty good one of the corpse and laid it on the table. Whitey glanced at it, bent down to take a forkful of tamale, looked at the picture again, then shot a reproachful glance at me.

"What's the idea, showing me a picture of a stiff?"

"Know her?" I asked.

He took a couple more mouthfuls, then studied the picture. He drank some coffee, wiped his mouth with his hand, wiped his hand on a paper napkin and picked up the picture.

"Looks familiar. I ain't sure—"

I held my breath. Singer stared intently at Whitey.

"You know her?" I asked finally.

Whitey dropped the picture and scratched the back of his head. He looked at me.

"I ain't sayin' for sure," he said. "But if it's the dame I'm thinkin' of, I know who she was."

I kept on holding my breath.

"I don't know if this is the one for sure. The one I'm thinkin' of— we called her 'Gandy.' Don't know any other name. She run a twenty-one game at a joint on the North Side. Place called the '7-11 Club.'"

CHAPTER ELEVEN

I talked Whitey into having dinner with us and we left the bar and went up to his room so he could change his clothes.

He was still living in a fifty-cent room in the neighborhood. I wondered why, since he looked more or less prosperous. But I didn't ask.

We climbed the stairs to the fourth floor and he found a key and unlocked the door. The room was bare and the bed was an old, lumpy brass job. There was no running water and the wallpaper was scratched and torn. But the place was clean. Whitey's shoes were lined up neatly along one wall. He'd always had trouble with his feet. Shoes were his only extravagance. In the old days he would buy shoes before food.

Singer sat down in the only chair and I leaned against the window sill.

Whitey took off his shirt and pants and shoes. He went into a little closet and came out with a tuxedo.

"Damn monkey suit!" he said, under his breath. "Only thing I don't like about this job."

"What's the job?"

"I'm floor manager at Race Cavanaugh's place on Rush Street."

Floor manager could only mean one thing. Whitey was a bouncer. From what I remembered and had heard about Race Cavanaugh's spot, the job must have kept him busy. But Whitey would love it. Give him a chance to rough guys up and still be "legitimate."

He was climbing into his monkey suit, swearing under his breath in a steady, monotonous flow of Irish profanity—which is the same as any other profanity, only more fervent.

"This babe in the picture," he said, interrupting himself, "she get knocked off?"

"Yeah."

"Where?"

"In our little town."

"Who done it?"

"We don't know. We're trying to find out."

Whitey looked at Singer.

"You a private eye?"

Singer was puzzled.

"A cop," Whitey said, "a shamus."

Singer smiled and shook his head.

"Just an amateur," I said. "This case involves an old friend of Singer's."

Whitey looked at me.

"Why would anybody want to be a cop—even an amateur?"

"Sometimes," I said, "you get forced into it."

Whitey had his shirt on and was looking for a tie in his dresser drawer.

"You going to check on this spot, this 7-11 Club?"

"Yeah," I said.

He gave me a look.

"Take it easy," he said. "That's a joe named Gantner. Tough. Very tough."

I rubbed the side of my face and nodded.

"I've had an introduction," I said.

"Every guy at Gantner's joint is a wronggo," Whitey said. "Every guy. Hatchet men all. The bastards."

"Funny," I said, "this dame in the picture—Candy—the cops didn't have a thing on her. Couldn't identify her."

"She was Gantner's girlfriend. He took good care of her." An unexpected murmur came from Singer.

"And yet, by heaven, I think my love as rare—"

Whitey looked at him, then at me.

"He okay?" Whitey asked.

I laughed.

"He's okay," I said.

"Let's go," Whitey said. "Where we goin'?"

"We'll go to our place, I guess. They've got a nice bar. Or we can get a bottle and go up to the room."

"That's okay," Whitey said "So I can eat and drink—what the hell!"

I held the door for Singer and followed him out. Whitey locked the door.

We went downstairs and out onto the street. I hailed a cab. Whitey tugged at my sleeve and spoke out of the corner of his mouth.

"You in the chips?" he said.

I nodded toward Singer.

"It's on him," I said.

Whitey looked at Singer and nodded. We got into the cab. I gave the driver the name of our hotel and he pulled away. We went a couple of blocks. Whitey seemed a little fidgety. He leaned forward and took hold of the front seat with his big hairy paws.

"Look, Mac," he said to the cabbie. "Drive around a couple of blocks, huh? Let's shake that shadow."

The cabbie glanced back.

"Uh-huh," he said. "I had a hunch."

He twisted the wheel sharply and we lurched to the left against a changing light. We went very fast for a block and a half, twisted suddenly right into an alley, came out a block later onto the street, turned left and somehow, in a way I never figured out, wound up on the lower level of Wacker Drive.

Whitey looked back through the rear window and so did I. It was dark and gloomy down there and there were cars behind us. I couldn't make anything out. But Whitey smiled and leaned back in his seat.

Singer said, "We are no longer being followed?"

"Not any more," Whitey said. "When did you first get wise?"

"About two hours ago," Singer said, "while Joseph and I were having lunch."

I looked at him.

* * * *

We stopped at a liquor store near the hotel and I got a couple bottles of whisky and some soda. We went up to the room. I called room service and ordered some glasses and ice. Singer slumped down on the sofa, stretching his long legs out, crossing his ankles. He closed his eyes. Whitey sat down with one leg over the arm of a chair. I was only halfway seated when there was a knock on the door of the adjoining room. It opened and Frank Stauffer came in, tiptoeing.

He looked tired, worn out. There were deep lines around his nose and mouth and his hair was rumpled.

He looked much older than usual. I felt sorry for him.

"Julia's in bed, asleep," he said. "I gave her a couple of sleeping tablets. She's had a rough time. Wouldn't talk much about it. Has an idea somebody's after her. She's scared."

Suddenly he noticed Whitey and stopped. I introduced them.

"Long time pal of mine," I said.

Frank nodded and turned back to Singer.

"Any luck?" he asked.

"No," Singer said. "But we haven't been here long."

Frank looked at Whitey, thought something over, then said, "I've got to get out and settle some—debts. Julia needs a long sleep. I wish you'd keep your eye on her. If you hear her moving around, go in and try to get her back to sleep. I told the desk not to accept any calls."

"Of course," Singer said.

There was a knock at the door. I went and took the glasses and ice from the bellboy, brought them back into the room and set them on the table. I opened one of the bottles.

"Have a drink," I said to Frank, "before you go."

He hesitated, then smiled a little and nodded.

"I could use it."

I dropped ice in the glasses, poured whisky over it and squirted some soda into each one. I handed them around. Whitey smelled his, grinned and drained it in one gulp. I opened the other bottle and handed it to him.

Frank Stauffer sat drinking slowly, frowning. He opened his mouth as if to say something a couple of times, seemed to think better of it and took another drink. Finally he got around to it.

"Singer," he said, "there's something I haven't told you. I guess I ought to. It's something I noticed last night when the sheriff went to the office with me to go through the Graves papers."

He stopped. He looked as if he wished he hadn't started it.

"Yes?" Singer said.

"Well—there's a paper missing. I didn't mention it to the sheriff. I wish I didn't have to mention it now. I promised to keep it a secret. But it's too late for that now, I guess."

"What sort of paper was it?" Singer asked.

"It was a map. A map of the Graves place, showing the location of something Seth Graves—put away; something he hid."

"What did he hide?"

"Fifty thousand dollars."

I whistled.

"Jesus!" said Whitey. He swallowed a drink the wrong way and coughed.

"It was for Linda," Frank said. "He told me—and I remember it very clearly—'Frank, I'm burying some money, for Linda, if she ever comes back. It probably looks silly. But nobody knows what will happen in fifteen or twenty years. I've known banks to go under, investments can turn out bad. I want this to be there, just in case.' He gave me the map. He'd buried the money himself and drawn the map and he told me to put it away and never mention it. I did, and I've never mentioned it—except to one person—before you."

"Who was that one?" Singer asked.

It took a long time for Frank to answer. When he did his voice was a hoarse whisper. "Julia."

He put his head down and covered his face with his hands. After a moment he looked up.

"Sorry," he said. "I don't know how much more of this I can take. I suppose the men who stole the corpse have it now."

"Why should they have it?" I asked.

"It's a logical conclusion," Frank said. "Julia must have taken the map and given it to Gantner, trying to stall him off. It's all of the same piece with the theory about her telling him the Graves place was available. She's been awfully desperate. Somehow, the map must have come into the possession of this woman who was killed. I don't understand it, but that's the only reason I can think of for her being there. Then, when they stole the body—"

Singer was nodding.

"It all fits," he said. "I might as well tell you we think we've identified the murder victim as a girlfriend of Gantner's."

Frank's eyes widened.

"You have? Then it's true. It must be. It's the only answer."

"Except," Singer said, "that the men who stole the body don't have the map."

"No?"

"No. I have it."

"You?"

Frank stared at him. Then he smiled and sighed in relief.

"That's a great load off my mind... I suppose you want to hold it for a while."

"If you don't mind," Singer said.

"There's something I don't get," I said.

"You ain't the only one," Whitey said, who looked dazed.

"We went out there and found that the dead woman had dug around in the dirt in several places. But she hadn't even come close to where it looked like the money was, according to the map."

Frank laughed.

"There's a trick to the map," he said. "A stranger to the Graves place could dig up three acres without finding it."

"Oh," I said.

Singer took the map out of his pocket.

"I can't tell you exactly where it is," Frank said. "I've still got to maintain a semblance of trust, on behalf of Linda. But I will give Singer a hint that I think he'll catch. You remember, Singer, the dog, Barcus?"

"Oh, yes," Singer said.

"You will notice that the directions on the map, at one point, say, 'Ten paces from Barcus' grave toward the corner of the barn nearest house.'"

Singer, who was following the map, nodded.

"When Barcus, the dog, was buried, it was toward the back of the lot, near the northeast corner. Linda buried him herself and put up a little stone marker. When Seth buried the money, he moved that marker, but made the directions actually from the grave itself. So only a person who knew the exact location of the real grave could find the exact spot. A stranger would take ten paces from the marker, which is not now anywhere near the dog's real grave. Linda would know the real grave—as I did."

I looked at Whitey.

"Have another drink," I said. "I'm going to."

"I can't help myself," Whitey said, taking a long pull from the bottle.

Frank looked at his watch.

"I've got to go," he said, rising. "Will you keep an eye on Julia? And please take good care of the map."

Singer smiled and nodded.

"I'll take good care of both of them," he said.

At the door, Frank turned back to Singer.

"Singer—I know it probably doesn't mean a thing, but—I'm convinced that even though Julia has apparently run riot with the Graves property and seems to be deeply involved with Gantner—she isn't guilty of the murder."

Singer looked a little cold. It was amazing. I almost didn't like him for a minute. He looked at Frank and said slowly, "I sincerely hope you are right."

Frank started to say something more, then changed his mind and went out. There was a long silence.

"Who's this dame Julia?" Whitey asked.

"A local woman," I said. "Frank's wife. A high-stepping kid. She keeps coming to Chicago and getting in trouble." Whitey thought it over.

"That must be some little town you guys have," he said. Singer smiled.

"It is really a quiet little town. It is only this sudden concentration of unfortunate circumstances that makes us appear crime-ridden."

"Oh, sure," Whitey said. "Tell me something about this murder."

We told him. I told part of it and Singer filled in. Whitey figured it out right away.

"Nothin' to it," he said. "One of Gantner's boys. Gantner knew this Candy went down there lookin' for somethin'. He found out what it was and had her knocked off. Then he went down there himself to look around. Or—maybe he knocked her off himself. But I don't think so."

Singer gazed at Whitey with admiration.

"Quite possible," he said. "You have an alert mind, Mr. Callahan. You think we ought to ask the Chicago police to pick up Mr. Gantner?"

"Well—no," Whitey said. "Not till you can pin something on him. And when you can, I don't want to be there."

Singer nodded.

"It is the search for something to pin on him that occupies us now."

Whitey shrugged.

"Any way you want to put it," he said.

I guess all three of us heard it at the same time. We all looked at each other and Whitey stopped his glass halfway to his mouth.

It was the sound of someone talking. A low, uncertain—sometimes excited—sound.

"Julia," I said, and Singer and I got to the door at the same time.

"Quietly," Singer said, as I turned the knob. "She may still be asleep."

We went in. The shades were drawn and the room was quite dark. One window had been raised a few inches and now and then the curtains fluttered in the breeze. A thin streak of sunlight crossed the sill and fell across the floor.

There was a double bed in the corner of the room. Julia Stauffer was in the bed. She was turning and tossing, throwing back the covers, or clutching them, and talking all the time. Singer and I stood beside the bed, watching and listening.

"Stay away..." she was saying, "...stay away from me, you hear?... Hear me? ...no, no!... I can't pay...my husband... Frank...Frank!" There was a dead silence, then her voice rose to a scream. "Frank!..."

There were footsteps and I whirled around. It was only Whitey, standing in the doorway with a drink in his hand.

Julia lay still for a few moments, breathing quietly, slowly. Then she got restless. Her breath came, faster and faster and more unevenly. She pushed the covers off and under her nightgown her big body writhed and twisted.

"Didn't tell them... Frank... Please! Didn't tell—how to read the map...Frank!"

She began to shiver. I reached down and pulled the blanket up over her.

"I've had enough of this," I muttered to Singer.

Julia had stopped talking. She still twisted and turned, but she didn't say anything.

"Maybe she'll quiet down now," I said.

Singer nodded and we moved away from the bed and tiptoed toward the door, where Whitey stood.

We didn't quite make it. There was a scream behind us.

"Frank!"

We both turned around.

She was sitting straight up in bed, her eyes open. We went back there. Her eyes stared straight ahead and at first she didn't seem to see us. Then her head turned slowly and she looked at us. I was closest and I reached out and put my hand on her shoulder.

She struck at me.

"Get away!" she said. "Get away from me!"

Singer leaned over the bed.

"Julia," he said softly, "it's all right. It's Singer Batts and Joe. Everything's all right."

She stared at Singer. Her face looked angry, then frightened. Her mouth twisted into a crooked line. She drew away and shrank against the wall.

"Singer Batts," she said, in a husky, dead-sounding voice. "What do you want?"

"I just came in to see that you were all right," Singer said.

"Go away," she said. "Get out. Get out of here!"

She crouched on the bed by the wall like a trapped animal, her gaze fixed on Singer's face. She looked as if she were waiting for Singer to drag out a gun and blast her.

I looked at Singer.

"All right, Julia," he said. "We're going. Try to get back to sleep."

This time we made it, all the way. We closed the door behind us and went into our own room.

CHAPTER TWELVE

We couldn't leave Julia, and we had to eat. I ordered dinner sent up, along with another bottle of whisky and some beer. Whitey had seemed to think the first bottle was his personal property, and I figured Singer needed a dividend.

"I'm gettin' the creeps," Whitey said. "You got a lot of very funny people mixed up in this shenanigans. What was that dame in there talking about?"

"I don't know," I said.

"Sounded like maybe she welshed on a loss at the tables and thought they was comin' to collect."

"No doubt," Singer said, "that is what Frank has gone to settle about."

"If she's been gamblin' with Gantner," Whitey said grimly, "he'd damn well better settle. Those boys will come and collect."

I looked at Singer. Singer looked at me.

Our dinner came up, with the bottle. Whitey unconsciously made a move for it, but I got there first and poured out half a tumbler of whisky and set it down beside Singer's plate. We ate silently. Whitey never talked when he ate and Singer was busy in his head.

We had nearly finished when we heard the latch click on the door connecting our rooms. Singer was facing the door. Whitey and I had to turn to see.

Julia Stauffer stood there in a long red dressing gown. Her hair was disheveled, her big face pasty and smeared with faint traces of rouge and lipstick. Her eyes were dull and tired.

"Got anything to drink?" she asked.

I got up, went to the table and mixed her a stiff one. She took it and stood there, leaning against the door, drinking it. She didn't say anything. I called room service and asked them to take our dinner table away.

Julia set her glass down and looked at the three of us.

"Who's that?" she asked, pointing at Whitey.

I told her.

"I'm sorry, Singer," she said, "about the way I talked to you in there. I'd been having a nightmare—"

"A nightmare—about me?" Singer asked.

"No. About—nothing. Just a nightmare. Why did Frank go off and leave me?"

"He said something about—settling some debts," Singer said.

Julia covered her face with her hands. Her hands were large, the skin coarse and freckled. She wore a lot of heavy rings. Her shoulders began to shake. She was crying.

I took her arm and led her to the sofa. She sat down. After a while she took her hands away. She was still crying, but she didn't seem to care.

"I'm in a mess," she said. "I'm in a hell of a mess. I guess.—I'm just naturally a messy person. You probably think so. Everybody in Preston thinks so."

"What's the trouble, Julia?" Singer asked.

"I've got reason," she said. "All my life, I've played second fiddle—to Linda Graves. I know Frank is still in love with her. There's nothing I can do about it. You don't know what it means—"

Nobody said anything. There wasn't a hell of a lot you could say.

"Did I talk in my sleep?" Julia asked suddenly.

"Yes," Singer said.

"What did I say?"

Singer didn't answer right away. He looked into space. Julia's face was strained.

"What did I say?"

Her voice was tight and thin. She spoke through her teeth.

"You talked about not being able to pay," Singer said. "You kept calling for Frank."

"Is that all? Didn't I say anything else?"

Another pause. Then Singer said, "One other thing. You said you had not told them about how to read the map."

She looked at me.

"Didn't I say anything else?" she asked.

"That's all," I said.

She had stopped crying. Her face was streaked with the tears that had run down her cheeks. She laughed a little. "I thought I must have talked for a couple of hours."

"It seems that way when you're sleeping," Singer said. "It was actually only for a few seconds. What do you suppose you meant by not telling them how to read the map?" She ignored the question.

"You could hear me way in here?" she said.

"Faintly."

"My God." She sighed, a long, shuddering sigh. Her head dropped against the back of the sofa. "Oh—my God!"

"Is there anything we can do for you, Julia?" Singer asked. "Is there any way we can help you?"

She laughed again, a short hard laugh and I figured Julia Stauffer was about at the end of her rope.

"Not unless you can pay my debts," she said. "I've got a hell of a lot of debts."

"How much do you owe Lloyd Gantner?" Singer asked.

"About ten thousand dollars. What do you know about Lloyd Gantner?" Her eyes were hardening into suspicious little spots in her face.

"Not as much as I'd like," Singer said. "Maybe you could tell us something about him."

Julia shook her head.

"I couldn't tell you anything about him."

"Could you tell me anything else, about anything?"

"Maybe," she said. "Why all the questions?"

"The day after our little murder in Preston," Singer said, "Lloyd Gantner came to town."

"To Preston?"

Julia's eyes widened.

"Did you know a woman named Candy?"

Julia looked at Singer and laughed a nasty little laugh. "Playing detective again?" she said.

I began to burn. Also I developed an idea. I gave Whitey a signal and we got up. I turned my back on Julia and winked at Singer and he got up.

"We'd better get going," I said. "Got a lot to do."

We all moved toward the door.

Julia stood up suddenly.

"Wait a minute!" she said. "Where are you going? You can't go now!"

I looked around.

"How's that?" I asked.

"You can't leave me here alone now. You can't—"

I nudged Singer and Whitey through the door. I went last, holding the knob.

"Wait!" Julia called.

I closed the door. Singer and Whitey walked a little way down the hall.

Julia was screaming at us now. I heard her run across the room and then her fists were pounding on the door. "Come back!" she said. "Please— come back!"

She grabbed the knob, twisted it and jerked open the door. I had moved on after Singer and Whitey. Julia stepped out in the hall.

"Singer!" she called. "Come back. Please, please, don't leave me."

Singer half-turned, hesitating.

"You can ask me all the questions you want to. All night long. Only, don't leave me."

She had begun to cry again. She was really in very bad shape.

We hadn't intended to leave her, of course, and I guess we'd made our point. We all walked back into the room. Whitey looked a little bewildered but he played along. There was still whisky left in his bottle.

We sat down again in the room.

"Have you played at Gantner's place in the past?" Singer asked.

"No. Just this time."

"This woman called Candy," Singer said. "Did you know her?"

"Candy?"

"Did you know her?"

"Not that I remember. May I have another drink?"

I got up and fixed one for her.

"This map you were talking about," said Singer. "What would that be?"

Julia lit a cigarette, took a long drag and studied her toes. Finally she looked straight at Singer.

She asked, "Has Frank told you anything about it?"

"Something, yes."

"Well, I couldn't add to that. If he told you anything, he told you all of it."

"Not quite. He didn't say how it came to be missing from his files."

"Didn't he guess?"

"He guessed that perhaps you had taken it."

Julia, looking him square in the eye, said, "That's right."

There was a pause. I felt as if we were right on the brink of a discovery, and yet were a thousand miles away from it.

"One more thing," Singer said. "The evening of the murder, early—the same evening you left for Chicago—Joseph went up to the Graves place to do a little investigating, of a friendly nature. Somebody stuck a note in the band of his hat. The note warned him to stay away from Linda Graves. At that time, of course, we all thought it was Linda who was staying in the house. Did you write that warning note?"

Frank Stauffer came into the room through the connecting door. He looked more beaten than ever.

"Julia," he said, "you ought to be sleeping."

"Couldn't," Julia said. "Singer has been hounding me about the murder."

"Singer—" Frank said, with some desperation.

"I haven't really been hounding you, have I, Julia?"

Julia shrugged. Now that Frank was here she didn't give a damn whether we stayed or not. Neither did I. Whitey looked restless and I thought we ought to go find Gantner. I guess Singer thought so, too.

"We'll have to run along," he said. "Is there anything we can do for you?"

Frank shook his head.

"No, thank you," he said.

We went out. As we walked down the hall Whitey said under his breath, "I got a strong hunch—a very strong hunch, that in about three weeks, that dame in there is going to be completely off her nut."

Singer didn't answer.

We got into the elevator and went down to the lobby. Singer left our key at the desk and we went out to the street.

Whitey had to go to work, so we walked over to Race Cavanaugh's place with him.

As he left us he said, "I wouldn't want to see you boys worry, but our little pal is back—the shadow."

"Thanks," I said. "So-long, Whitey."

"I'll drop in later. Maybe it'll be more excitin'," he said.

"Doubtless," murmured Singer.

"Take it easy with Gantner," Whitey said, "and try to find out who the tail is. You might want to know."

He went into Race's place, and I said, "Let's walk a few blocks."

"Anything you wish," Singer said, he was thinking very hard. We walked, without talking, up Rush Street to some cross lane and back to Michigan. It was an off hour and we were practically alone.

I clutched at Singer's sleeve as we passed a drugstore and we went in. I bought a pack of cigarettes and stalled around a minute and then we stepped outside again. Just as we hit the sidewalk a cab went by slowly, almost at a walking pace, close to the curb.

A guy sat in the back seat. As he passed us he struck a match to light a cigarette, but the way his hands were cupped around it, I couldn't see his face.

CHAPTER THIRTEEN

We got into a cab, gave the driver the address of the 7-11 Club.

"If we're being followed," I said, "we must have been followed all the way from Preston."

"You think Mr. Gantner is following us?"

"Not personally, but—who else?"

"I don't know."

"Shall we try to shake him?"

"Not now. We are not on any nefarious errand."

"It's not our errand I'm worried about."

"Let's not worry about it at all, right now. What did you think of Julia?"

"I'm glad I haven't been married to her for twenty-five years."

"Do you think she was telling the truth?"

"I don't think Julia would know the truth at this stage of her life, not even if it kicked her in the face."

"A harsh judgment, Joseph."

"I'm a harsh guy."

Singer didn't say anything. I guess I really am a harsh guy in some ways. But then, I've led a harsh life.

"Look," I said. "Suppose Julia tried to write off her gambling debts by giving Gantner the map showing where the fifty thousand bucks are hidden. Then he sent this girlfriend, Candy, down to Preston to look the place over. When Candy found she couldn't locate the money—and maybe even doubted that it was really there—she told Julia she'd have to pay up, and so there was only one more thing for Julia to do."

"You like to think that Julia killed her?"

"I don't like to think anybody would kill anybody, but that makes sense."

Singer thought it over. After a long time he said, "I admit it makes a certain sort of sense."

We were riding out North Sheridan Road now and ahead was the top of the Edgewater Beach Hotel. We came to a section of small stores and shops, a few taverns and delicatessens. The cabbie slowed down. I saw a canopy over the sidewalk with "7-11 Club" in six inch letters on it. The driver made a U-turn and came up on the right side in front of the canopy.

"Kind of early, ain't it?" he asked.

"Yeah," I said. "Cold, too. We'll hang around."

"Okay."

I paid him and we got out. He drove away I looked at my watch. It was seven-thirty.

"We can get a drink," I said. "Maybe Gantner comes to work early."

We went to the door! As Singer stepped in ahead of me, I glanced back at the street. A cab had drawn up on the other side, a little way down and a guy was climbing out. I followed Singer inside.

It was a small place, dimly lighted. There was a short, curved bar on one side and the rest of the room was taken up with tables. In one corner was a little platform with three or four music stands and a small piano. There was a dance floor about ten feet square. Like a thousand other spots in town.

Nobody sat at the tables. There was one guy at the bar. Two bartenders in white jackets leaned against the back of the bar, looking bored. Now and then one or the other of them would step over to the bar and flick at it with a rag. But there wasn't anything to flick.

We sat down at the bar and ordered rye highballs. There wasn't any rye, so we took bourbon. There wasn't any bourbon, either, and whatever it was, there wasn't enough of it to make the glass worth lifting. I ordered another one, double. It tasted like the first one. I tried once more. When the bartender set it down I asked, "Mr. Gantner in?"

"I don't know," he said.

"We'd like to see him."

He hesitated.

"I'm not sure he's in, Mac. If he is—Mr. Gantner's a very busy man."

"No doubt," I said.

I pulled from my pocket one of our business cards. It read: *HOTEL PRESTON*. Singer *Batts, Prop. Joe Spinder,* Mgr. I handed the card to the bartender.

He looked at it, twisted his mouth a little, dropped it back on the bar. He shook his head.

"Like I say—Mr. Gantner's a very busy man."

Singer cleared his throat.

"My good man," he said, in his thinnest, tightest voice, "I do not enjoy your conversation any more than I like your whisky. I want to see Mr. Gantner. If you will inform him that we are here to discuss the *candy* situation with him, I am sure he'll see us. As a matter of fact, I believe that if you don't get that message to him, and he finds later that we were here, he will be extremely unpleasant about it."

The bartender stared at Singer. Then something that creeps into Singer's tone of voice when he gets his mind set went to work on him. He went over to the other bartender, said something to him and disappeared through a door at the far end of the room. He was gone for about five minutes.

While he was gone, a guy came in and sat down at the end of the bar and ordered a beer. I got a look at him when he glanced up at the bartender and the light fell on his face. He was broad and flat-nosed and stupid looking. Exactly the kind of a guy who could sneak around behind you without raising any suspicions.

The bartender came back and leaned over the bar.

"Go through the door at the back marked Private," he said. "Turn to the right. There's a door marked Office. Mr. Gantner is in."

"Thank you," Singer said.

We got off our stools and went to the rear door. As I reached out to push it, it swung open and there was a guy standing behind it. He wore a tuxedo and he looked about as happy in it as Whitey looked in his. He was a thickset, bull-necked guy, with black hair that crawled down low on his forehead.

"This way," he said, and I wondered how a gorilla would sound if he could talk.

We followed him down a short corridor to the door marked Office. The guy knocked a couple of times, twisted the knob and opened the door. We went in and he stayed outside.

There was a big desk, the top clean and polished, with no papers lying on it. There was a sofa and an overstuffed armchair. There were some paintings on the wall. They looked pretty good to me, though I don't know anything about art.

Gantner was sitting behind the desk, leaning back, his hands resting on the edge of the desk. He smiled.

"Gentlemen," he said, in a silky voice, "what can I do for you?"

Singer returned the smile—he always does. I didn't. Gantner noticed it and laughed.

"I'm sorry I had to hit you so hard," he said to me. "I was—in a hurry."

"Forget it," I said. "The next time I'll be ready."

"Are you sure?" he asked, looking me over.

I didn't like the way he said it, but I didn't want to interfere with anything Singer had in mind so I let it pass.

Gantner looked at Singer.

"You had something to ask me?"

Singer kept smiling.

"You anticipate me."

"I try to. You want to know what I was doing in your town."

"No," Singer said. "We want to know who it was who started you thinking about our town."

"Let's just say it was a little bird."

"How much money does Julia Stauffer owe you?" Gantner's easy smile went away. His lips tightened. These things themselves were barely noticeable, but they changed his face entirely. It was a mean face.

"Nine thousand eighty-seven dollars," he said.

"I understood her husband was coming to settle up with you," Singer said.

Gantner's head moved slightly.

"I have not seen her husband. I don't know who he is. All I know is that the debt still stands."

"I take it that Mrs. Stauffer owed you at least nine thousand dollars before you went to Preston the other day."

"You go ahead," Gantner said. "You're doing all right."

"Perhaps I will be doing you a service if I tell you that the Graves place is not now and never was worth nine thousand dollars."

Gantner looked puzzled. "Well?" he said.

I was a little puzzled, too, but I managed to keep it to myself.

"I assumed," Singer said, "that it had been represented to you as having at least that value."

"Not in itself—no," Gantner said.

"Not in itself? For something connected with it, or buried in it—is that it?"

Gantner smiled again.

"I've nothing more to say. If that's all, you'll have to excuse me."

"Mr. Gantner." Singer's voice was hard and sharp. "I am on a serious errand. We know the identity of the woman who was murdered at the Graves place. We know that you were in Preston yourself. I have a variety of clues, all of which lead to this office. If I cannot get my answers from you in this fashion, I will expect the police to get them for me—in their fashion."

Gantner had stopped smiling. He leaned forward, both his hands flat on his desk.

"I'm serious too," he said. "Suppose you answer a question for *me*. It is possible—is it not?—for a person driving a fast car, to take the county road north out of Preston, drive to Preston junction, turn right on a private road that runs for a mile to the east, then angles south and west to a point one-quarter mile behind and east of the Graves house; it is possible to do this, remain for—as long as necessary—return to the car and retrace the path to Preston Junction and get on Highway 98 to Chicago; to do this with very little loss of time and with practically no chance of being noticed. I say it's possible. Am I right?"

"Whether or not you are right has nothing to do with what I am saying," Singer told him. "As an extortionist and blackmailer of some repute, you have undoubtedly studied the penalties for those operations. I am serving notice on you that I am prepared to have you arrested on specific charges and thrown into jail."

I think Singer was going to say something more, but he didn't quite get around to it. There was a slight grating sound, as if a drawer had been opened suddenly and Gantner was standing straight behind his desk, and in his right hand was a small, shiny automatic. It pointed straight at Singer's stomach. Gantner's face was twitching a little and his eyes were half-closed.

"You jerkwater Sherlock," he said between his teeth. "That's the last thing you'll ever say to me—or anybody else."

Singer just smiled at him.

Everything happened very fast then. I was standing near the door, facing Gantner, where I'd been standing ever since we went in. There was a light switch on the wall beside the door. I readied behind me for the light switch and yelled to Singer, "Drop." I guess he did, because I heard the thud before I heard the shot and in the dark saw the flash of Gantner's automatic.

I made it around the desk from memory, barking one shin on a chair as I passed.

Gantner was easy to find. I slugged him as hard as I could and groped for his right hand. He fell and I went down on top of him, grabbed the gun and got up as the light went on and our pal the gorilla stood there in the doorway.

For thirty seconds it was a stalemate—the gorilla and me, each with a gun. Then something hit Gorilla very hard in the belly. It was Singer's foot. It hit him so hard that the guy doubled over, grunted and dropped his gun.

I beat it around the desk again, retrieved the gun and stuck it in my pocket. Gantner had climbed to his feet and was glaring at me with much hatred.

"Like I said," I told him. "Next time I would be ready." He didn't say anything.

"I'll mail the guns back to you—sometime," I said, dropping the second one into my other pocket. They felt very heavy, very good.

Singer opened the door and we went out. We found the door marked Private and walked rapidly through the bar to the street. A cab was coming and we got in.

"I think our next move," I said, "is to get out of town by the shortest possible route."

"Soon," Singer said. "We have one or two more things to look into."

I felt a small cold wind on the back of my neck.

CHAPTER FOURTEEN

Singer told the cabbie to stop at a drugstore and wait and we got out and went in to the phone booths. Singer called the hotel. There was a message saying, "Call Ashland 7007 for news of Linda Graves."

Singer immediately dialed the number, waited and in a moment was talking to someone. I watched through the dull glass in the door of the booth. I couldn't hear anything that was said.

Singer hung up and opened the door. His face was excited. Without a word he went out and climbed into the cab. I followed him. He gave the cabbie an address out on the west side and told him to hurry. I leaned back in the seat and prayed that Gantner wouldn't think we were worth the trouble of vengeance.

We rode for fifteen minutes, the cabbie taking dark side streets to avoid traffic. Finally he pulled up before a dingy, dark building under a sign that read, *James Pullman, Mortician.*

"Shall I wait?" the cabbie asked.

"Please," Singer said.

We walked up the steps, lighted by a feeble, yellow bulb, to the door of the place. There was a bell handle you had to twist. Singer twisted it and we heard it ring. We waited quite a while and Singer rang again. Then we heard footsteps and the door opened slightly. A short guy with a bald head peered out at us.

"I am Singer Batts. I spoke to you over the telephone a few minutes ago."

"Oh, yes. Come in, please."

He opened the door enough for us to get inside and as soon as we'd made it, closed it quickly and bolted it. He led the way down a short corridor to a door marked Office and stood back for us to go in. It was a dingy little office with an old-fashioned rolltop desk and some straight chairs. The walls were covered with photographs of people I didn't recognize and the desk was littered with papers. The floor hadn't been swept for a long time.

He was a funny-looking little guy and very nervous. He kept looking beyond us, as if expecting somebody else any minute. I didn't want anybody else myself. I liked it better when we were at least two against one.

He sat down at his desk and pointed out two chairs to us. We sat down, too, and waited.

He fussed with some papers and hemmed and hawed around for a while. His fingers were short and grimy. I wouldn't have wanted him to work on me even after I was dead.

"I read your ad in the paper," he said. "I'm taking an awful chance, calling you. It can get me in a lot of trouble. If I were sure—"

"I won't betray you," Singer said, "you can be sure—unless you've committed some obvious crime—"

The little bald head shook vigorously.

"Oh, no. Nothing like that. A slight little irregularity, maybe, but no crime—nothing like that."

"What was it you had to tell us?"

"Well—I—it's about this Linda Graves."

"Yes?"

"I thought—maybe it might be—"

He couldn't come right out with it.

"How much?" Singer asked.

The guy made a little gesture.

"Now, I don't want you to think I'm trying to shake you down—"

"How much?"

"Say—a thousand dollars?"

His little eyes moved around restlessly. When nobody said anything he looked appealingly at us.

"Five hundred?"

"I will give you twenty-five dollars for your trouble," Singer said, "and another twenty-five if it turns out to be the Linda Graves in whom I'm interested."

"Well, now—"

Singer got up from his chair.

"All right," the little guy said in a hurry. "All right. I really think it's worth more than that. But, it's sort of on my conscience—you're not detectives, are you?"

His eyes were suddenly frightened.

"No," Singer said. "This is entirely a private affair." Singer practically never lied to anybody about anything. When he did, it was always perfect.

"Well," Baldy said, "early this morning, about two-thirty, two men came in and told me their sister had died and would I come and—arrange things. I went with them and found that there wasn't very much to arrange. The deceased had apparently already been embalmed and was dressed for burial. I thought at the time that the embalming job had been a bad one. I asked why they had come to me and they explained that the mortician who had started the case had been taken ill suddenly and they wanted to finish it up and have her cremated."

"It was all rather mysterious, wasn't it?" Singer asked. "Wouldn't you normally look into something like that a little further?"

Baldy looked at his dirty nails.

"Yes, of course," he said. "But they had papers—a birth certificate identifying her as Linda Graves, age forty-six; they had a death certificate that stated she had died of heart failure."

"Do you recall what the birth certificate said in regard to her place of birth?"

"Yes—it was some town in the next state, a town called Preston."

"Can you describe the two men who came to you?"

"I could, but I'd rather not. It doesn't have anything to do with Miss Graves and they were rather rough characters. I don't like to think of their finding out—"

"Very well. You made arrangements then to cremate this person?"

"Yes. It was done this afternoon."

"How much did the men pay you?"

"Two thousand dollars."

Singer reached in his pocket and pulled out a photograph of Candy, one of those taken at the scene of the crime. He laid it on the desk.

"Was this the woman?" he asked.

Baldy studied the picture. Then he looked at Singer and nodded.

"Yes," he said. "That's the one."

Singer said, "Give Mr. Pullman fifty dollars, Joseph."

I thought we were being robbed, but I reached for my wallet. My hand was halfway to the pocket when I heard the swish of the door behind me and felt a rush of air. I was about to turn, when I noticed Baldy's face. It was as white as milk and scared, more scared than I have ever seen any man's face get. He was staring over my head at the doorway. Then he got out of his chair, very slowly, and backed away, inch by inch till he ran into the far wall and couldn't go any farther. He stayed there, crouched down a little, his hands pressed flat against the wall.

I decided I might as well look around.

I'd seen both of them before, and not long before. Big guys, with padded shoulders and hats and poker faces. Only this time they both had guns.

"Well, well," I said, feeling sick, but too foolish to admit it. "This job is taking quite a lot of your time, isn't it?"

"Shut up!" one of the guys said. "Get up with your hands up and walk out of here. You, too," he said to Singer. "And frisk 'em," he ordered his pal.

And the two guns in my pockets were just beginning to feel at home. I swore while they moved to a new one.

"Shut up!" the guy said.

Singer and I got up and stepped out of the office. The one who had spoken followed us, kicked the door shut with his heel, leaving the other hood inside with the bald undertaker. We stood there. I heard a couple of swishing sounds and then Baldy screaming. That only lasted a few seconds. Then there were some loud thumps. The other guy opened the door and came out of the office, putting his gun away.

"Funny," he said, "I guess he's dead. I didn't know he was that soft."

"Shut up," the other mug said.

Those seemed to be about the only words he knew.

The guy who had taken care of Baldy turned and walked toward the front door. The other one prodded me in the back with his gun .

"Get moving," he said.

I nodded at Singer and we followed the first guy outside. There was a big car parked out front. It looked like the same car that had been used for the corpse snatch in Preston, but I couldn't be sure. The first guy opened the back door of the car and motioned to us to get in. Singer got in first and I followed. The guy who still had the gun climbed in and sat down beside me, pulling the car door shut behind him. The other guy got behind the wheel. It was all very, very familiar, as if I'd done it all before—only this time I was more nervous.

The motor roared and we lunged forward on the dark street.

"This is fun," I said, "but we didn't figure on it."

"No use talkin' to me," the gunman said. "I don't know nothin'."

"All right."

I sat there, trying to figure out a way to signal Singer to open the door if we ever slowed down. I didn't like the thought of having to jump, but I didn't like the thought of taking this ride either. Then I noticed that there wasn't any handle on the door on Singer's side, so it didn't really matter.

Anyway, we weren't slowing down. I hadn't paid much attention to our route on the way out here, so I didn't know where we were and I didn't know in what direction we were heading. The driver knew, though. We took side streets and didn't hit a single light.

But it took a long time. We kept going and going, and I didn't know where. Even when we got there I didn't know. It was a big building on a very dark street. There were other big buildings and they all looked about the same. They looked like warehouses, or maybe they were stores that had been converted.

We stopped in front of this place and the guy with the rod got out and beckoned to us. I couldn't see any lights in the building. The driver got out and we started our little parade again, the driver, then Singer and me and behind us the joe with the gun.

The guy led us up to the building. There was a wide entrance under a little canopy. The doors had no glass in them. The guy pushed a button at one side of the doors and waited. I counted to twenty. Then the door opened and we walked inside.

We were in a wide, dark corridor. There was a dim light in the ceiling about halfway along. At the far end, straight ahead, was a stairway.

Our footsteps in the corridor sounded loud, echoing. We were all walking in step, with the same beat, making the same time. I decided to experiment. I slowed down slightly, so that little by little I dropped behind Singer and got out of step.

It took only a few seconds. The guy in back jammed that stiff little round object into the middle of my back and said, "Stick to the pace, bud."

"Sorry," I said. "I got a sore foot."

"That's tough," he said.

We got to the stairs and started to climb. They were shallow steps and there were a lot of them. We reached one landing, turned and got to the next floor, then started up again toward the third floor.

On the third floor landing we turned away from the stairs and went down another corridor. We went about twenty feet and came to a door. No light showed around it and the only way I knew it was a door was that it had a knob on one side.

One of the mugs knocked on the door three times and somebody inside said, "Come in."

He opened the door and went inside and we followed.

This was a large room with an overhead light in the center, a huge table, about chest high, and nothing else. The light hung over the middle table.

Sitting on the edge of the table, kicking his heels slowly back and forth, was the gorilla from Gantner's office. He was still wearing the tuxedo, but it didn't seem to be bothering him now. His big head was ducked down into his bull neck and he looked at us out of little eyes.

The guy with the gun closed the door and he and the other guy went to the table and leaned against it. The gorilla sitting on it looked at us for a long time.

"Which one of you is Batts?" he asked.

"I am," Singer said.

The gorilla looked at one of the mugs who had brought us.

"You locked the door, Jerry?" he asked.

Jerry was the one who'd carried the gun. He nodded.

Gorilla looked at Singer again.

"Where's the map?" he said.

"The map?" Singer said, his innocent eyes looking wide.

"You know what map I mean. Where is it?"

"I don't have the slightest idea," Singer said. "I'm not carrying it."

Gorilla looked at me.

"Where is it?" he asked.

I figured Singer had it in his pocket and since I didn't see what they could do with it if they had it, it didn't seem very important to me. But Singer had given me the lead and I had to stick to it.

"Cut it out," I said. "Didn't you have enough trouble with us in Gantner's office?"

He quit kicking his feet back and forth and slid down off the table. It was quite a slide, because the table was high and he was short, but he did it without much trouble, he was catlike on his feet. He walked up to us and stared at Singer for a while, then at me, then back at Singer.

"Just answer the questions," he said.

His voice was too quiet. It made me sore.

"Shut up!" I said. "I'm sick of this. If we did know, we wouldn't tell you."

"If I don't hear what I want to," he said, "you'll be a lot sicker before you leave—if you leave."

He looked at Singer once more.

"The Stauffer dame gave the map to Gantner," he said. "Gantner gave it to Candy. Candy went down there and somebody killed her. Gantner went down to get the map back and couldn't get near the place or Candy. We got Candy, but the map wasn't on her."

"It's fun, searching a stiff, isn't it?" I asked.

The little eyes turned on me slowly, measured me, then looked away.

"Where's the map?" he said, and I knew he was asking it for the last time.

"This is a waste of time," Singer said. "I am trying to find the murderer of Candy. I know nothing of any map. I don't have time to discuss it, and I'm afraid I'll have to ask you to excuse me."

This would have been funny at almost any other time. Somehow, it wasn't funny at the moment.

Singer turned and started for the door. Behind him, Gorilla started to laugh. It was a low, hollow laugh that said, "Go ahead, bud—try it."

I started after Singer. The next thing I knew, something hit me in the back of the neck and I fell on my face. It stunned me and I crawled up to my knees and shook my head to clear it. Still on my knees, I looked around over my shoulder.

They'd knocked Singer down, too. But he was up now, up and with two mugs on each side of him, holding him. His head was sagging.

The gorilla was doing some more talking.

"Where's the map?" he said.

Singer didn't answer. There was a sharp crack, that sounded like a board slapping wet cement. Still Singer said nothing. By this time he probably couldn't.

My head was clearing a little. It still hurt, but I could see straight—and most of what I saw was a deep red.

"All right, Jerry," Gorilla said.

I watched over my shoulder. Jerry and his pal jerked Singer over to the table and propped him against its edge. I noticed Jerry wasn't carrying his gun now. That would help.

Gorilla reached in his pocket and pulled out a nail file, he leaned against the edge of the table and cleaned his fingernails. The white light over the table made him look pale. It threw long shadows across the floor.

I had to move sooner than I had planned. Still a little dazed, I was gazing over my shoulder at what was going on when the gorilla glanced at me. He dropped the nail file back into his pocket and took a couple of steps. Just then Jerry slugged Singer. He slugged him on the right side of his jaw and pushed up at the same time so that Singer's head snapped backward. Singer slumped against the table and Jerry's pal jerked him back up again and shook him.

Gorilla was moving in on me, reaching in his pocket again for what couldn't be a nail file. I turned and dived at his feet, without paying much attention to where I was going. The side of my face rubbed against his knee and I dug my face into the floor. He was down all right, but he was getting up fast.

I grabbed his ankle. He kicked it loose and got away. I got on my feet just in time to see him get that rod out of his pocket and try to sock me with it. I ducked and he swung over my head. I hit him in the stomach with all I had and he grunted and doubled over.

The other guys had looked around and Jerry came over to help Gorilla.

About that time I went nuts. I remember grinning at Jerry and saying, "You dirty bastard," and then he was all over me.

I was on the floor. I rolled out from under him and pushed and somehow got on top of him. Then the other mug grabbed my shoulders and pulled me off and I was down again with both of them on top of me. I saw Gorilla standing up, watching. I couldn't see Singer.

I kicked one of them—I don't know which—and he hollered and the other one slugged me in the face. I went blind for a minute and then they were dragging me to my feet, propping me against the table like they had Singer.

Singer was lying on the floor a little way off. He looked dead. He looked so dead that I started to cry and I broke away from one of the guys and kicked him in the groin. He sat down on the floor. The other one hit me in the face and I hit back at him, missed, lost my balance and fell down. He picked me up and I kicked him in the belly. He sat down. But by this time the other one was up and I couldn't win. He got me pinned against the table. Gorilla lifted his gun and hit me in the face with it. It struck the bridge of my nose and I gave up. I just stood there, feeling the pain and the rage and the fact that Singer was lying there and altogether it was the worst moment of my life. Gorilla was talking to me.

"You're foolish," he said. "All we wanted was a little information. We didn't want to hurt nobody. Why don't you tell us where the map is? Then we'll let you go."

I tried to say something, but couldn't.

He put his hand on my shoulder.

"It's simple," he said. "Just where the map is."

"I don't know where it is," I said. "For Christ's sake!"

He stared into my face for a long time. Then he said, "You know—I think maybe you're telling me the truth. I think maybe you don't know."

"What shall I do—write it in blood?" I said.

"There's only one thing. I'd be glad to let you go now. Only I just thought of something. Maybe you remember things. I guess maybe I talked too much. I wouldn't like for you to remember—this—and about stealing that corpse, and all that."

"Quit it," I said. "You've already finished him off—" I nodded toward Singer. "You might as well make it a full house."

The guy lifted his eyebrows.

"Him? He's all right. He don't feel so good right this minute. But he's alive. Don't worry about him."

I didn't know whether to believe him or not, so I kept still.

"The nice thing about this room," he said, "is that it's airtight, sound-proof." He looked around. So did I.

There were four window openings, but they were covered with steel plates. There was no transom over the door. "No sound," he said, "no smell."

I looked at him.

"There's nothing to it," he said. "It's almost too easy."

"What about when they find us?" I asked.

He laughed.

"That will be a long time."

"What if I told you where the map is?" He laughed again.

"It's too late, I think. You already told me you don't know."

All this time he had been playing with his gun, running his fingers up and down the barrel, polishing the butt with the heel of his hand. Now he slid it into his right hand and backed away toward the door.

"Mac," he said, "get Mr. Batts on his feet."

Mac walked over to where Singer lay on the floor.

"Get up," he said.

Singer didn't move. Mac kicked him in the chest. Singer rolled over.

I glanced at Gorilla, whose gun now pointed straight at my belt. He was too far away for me to get to him. If he shot me, he'd shoot Singer, too. Anyway, it looked as if he would shoot both of us, no matter what.

I waited. Mac, unable to get any response out of Singer, had bent over and got one arm under Singer's shoulders, he pulled Singer's left arm up and put it over his own shoulder. He raised up and Singer was on his feet. Mac half-carried, half-pushed him over to the table. He stepped back and slapped Singer's face.

Singer's eyes fluttered. His head turned toward me.

"Joseph," he said in a whisper. "What are these ruffians about?"

I couldn't look at him.

"They are about to shoot us," I said.

"Why?"

"Because we didn't tell them where the map is."

"Suppose we tell them."

"They won't believe us."

"I see."

"Maybe I should have spent more time in church," I said.

Singer smiled.

"Don't worry about it, Joseph."

"I'm not worried," I said. "I'm just not quite ready."

A low nasty laugh came from near the door. Gorilla was talking.

"Just to give you time to get ready," he said, "I'll count to ten."

He started to count. I glanced at Singer out of the corner of my eye. That peaceful smile was still on his face. He was probably somewhere with Shakespeare.

"…seven…eight…"

The gorilla's gun was level and steady. It looked like me first. Mac and Jerry stood behind him, Mac with his hand on the doorknob.

"…nine…"

When the noise came I braced myself all over, then couldn't understand why I didn't feel anything. There were reports, two of them, very loud. But I didn't feel anything. Nothing hit me.

I opened one eye and looked at Singer. He was still standing there, smiling. I opened the other eye, looked toward where the big shot with his two pals had been the last time I looked.

They were still there, but they weren't looking at us any more. They were looking at the door, from either side of it. Mac had his gun out now, too, and he was aiming at the door, the way Gorilla was aiming at it from the other side. Jerry stood behind Mac, waiting.

There was a dead pause, during which I listened to my heart beating, wondering whether it was showing through my coat and trying to figure out whether I could jump Mac in two long steps. I decided I couldn't.

Then a voice came from the other side of the door. It was a heavy, rumbling voice and it had a big ring of authority. It sounded good.

"Police," it said. "Open up and come out peaceful."

Mac looked at the gorilla.

"Don't open it," Gorilla said.

"There's a gang of 'em," Mac said.

"Hell, no."

"There was two guns at least," said Jerry. "Two different guns. I heard 'em."

There was a pounding on the door.

"I'll count three," the voice from the other side said. "Come on out—slow."

Mac shrugged and slipped his gun in his pocket. Gorilla wheeled and snarled at him. I couldn't make out his words, but Mac readied in and got his gun out again fast.

"…two…three," came the voice.

Then a shoulder hit the door from the other side. Something splintered. The thud came again and the door was loose. Gorilla stepped back along the wall and held his automatic on the door. Mac stepped back, too. This was fine. Singer and I would be the first available targets when the door opened.

Something hit the door again and that was all it took. I made up my mind. As the door toppled, I kicked at Singer's legs and he fell flat in front of the table. I ducked at the same time and threw myself across the floor, rolling toward Mac's legs. As I went, something zinged over my head and there was a sharp, splintering crack from the table top.

I never got to Mac's legs. I rolled up behind him, but he was already on the floor. He wasn't moving. I felt of him to make sure he wasn't going to move and he felt dead.

You think it was too soon for him to feel dead? Try it sometime. I felt a little dead myself, but not enough. I'd hit my head when I rolled over the floor and my eyes weren't focusing.

I rolled over slowly and got to my knees. I stuck one hand on Mac's neck and pushed myself up. My hand was sticky. I looked and saw that it was covered with blood.

Gorilla was standing over by the table, with his hands up to his shoulders. Jerry stood next to him, looking sheepish. Singer had got up and was doing something very unusual, for Singer. He was going through the pockets of Gorilla and Jerry, looking for concealed weapons. He did it gingerly, apologetically. You could see he didn't like to inconvenience anybody, even a guy who had been about to murder him.

I looked around to see who had brought all this about. I expected to see a corps of Chicago's finest grouped in the doorway, glowering.

There was one guy. He was a squat, broad-nosed guy, who might have been a butcher or maybe he ran a little dry-cleaning shop somewhere. Only now he didn't look especially stupid. He looked pretty sharp.

I was shaking my head to clear it and he saw me and grinned.

"Just like a movie," he said.

"Just too goddamned much like a movie," I said. "Brother, I'm sorry for all those nasty thoughts I had about you."

He looked hurt.

"You did? About me?"

In dry, meticulous tones, Singer Batts said, "They have no other weapons."

"Good," the guy said. "Let's get out of here."

He jerked his elbow at Gorilla and Jerry.

"Scram!" he said. "We'll follow you." He looked down. "We'll have to send a wagon to pick up your pal here." Gorilla and Jerry walked across the room and out the door. Singer and I followed and Broad-nose came last. He had knocked the door clear off the hinges. We walked over it to get out.

We went down the corridor to the stairway and Broad-nose caught up with Singer and me and watched Gorilla and Jerry walk downstairs.

"Good thing you pulled that dive," he said to me. "Where'd you learn that?"

"Right in that room," I said, "just at that time."

"This guy"—he nudged the gun toward Gorilla's back—"got nervous and turned to take a shot at you. That fixed it for his pal on the other side, of the door."

Singer hadn't said anything since we left the room. Now he turned to Broad-nose.

"We owe you a great deal," he said. "May I ask your name?"

"Brown," the guy said. "Peter Brown. Homicide. McMichaels assigned me to keep an eye on you guys. How you come to be playin' cops and robbers?"

"It's a long story," Singer said. "I'm sure it would bore you."

"Probably," Brown said.

We got out to the street and there was a car parked out in front, behind the one that had brought us.

"You drive?" Brown asked me.

"Sure," I said, climbing in behind the wheel.

"Excuse me a moment, please," said Singer, going over to the big black sedan belonging to the hoods.

He opened the back door, disappeared and then came out again, sticking something in his pocket. He climbed into the front seat with me, while Brown herded Jerry and Gorilla into the back seat.

"What did you forget?" I asked Singer.

"The map," he said. "I hid it beside the seat while we were riding over here."

I sighed.

"Headquarters?" I asked Brown.

"Uh-uh," he said. "We're going back to your hotel. Had a call just before I went in after you. Got to go by your hotel right away. Something happened to some dame back there—woman named Julia Stauffer."

I looked at Singer. He was staring straight ahead.

CHAPTER FIFTEEN

I didn't waste any time getting back to the hotel. During the ride Brown tried to get something out of Jerry and Gorilla, but they weren't having any. He quit it after a while and Singer told him something about the case that had got us into all this.

"I think I heard about you before," Brown said to Singer. "There was some murder back in your town a couple of years ago—some school teacher got knocked off. Right?"

"Right," I said.

"Why don't you come up here and join the force?"

"I'm afraid I'd make a poor policeman," Singer said.

"We all make poor policemen," Brown said, "till the case breaks."

"You were all right in there tonight," I said.

"Hell," Brown said. "Routine."

"Drive around in back," he said. "We've got to drag these two mugs along and it wouldn't look right takin' them through the lobby."

For the first time, Gorilla said something.

"Where do you get off takin' us to a hotel?" he said. "When do I call my lawyer?"

"Shut up!" Brown said. "We might need you. Looks like you boys have been pretty busy tonight."

We got out of the car in the rear of the hotel and went in the service entrance. There was a freight elevator just inside the door. We got in it and Brown pushed the button for our floor. Jerry and the gorilla stood there, glum and quiet. They were right. I wouldn't have trifled with this Peter Brown.

We went down the hall to our room, but Brown passed it up and went to the door of Frank Stauffer's room, adjoining. He knocked sharply with the butt of his .38. The door opened.

Inside were Frank Stauffer, two guys who looked like cops, another guy who looked tired and harassed and Whitey. Whitey sat on the edge of the bed, holding a fifth of gin, now and then taking a pull from it. Frank Stauffer sat in a chair at the desk. He was in his shirtsleeves and he kept rubbing his neck, as if it hurt him. He smiled wryly at Singer and me.

Singer looked bad. His eyes were puffy and he had a couple of blue blotches on his face and neck. I probably didn't look so good myself.

Whitey got up from the bed, carrying the bottle and came over and looked at us. He looked unhappy.

"Who's been beatin' you up?" he asked.

He handed me the bottle. I took a drink. He handed it to Singer, who shook his head.

The tired-looking guy spoke to us.

"I'm Masterson, from the D.A.'s office," he said. "We got a call from Mr. Stauffer here about half an hour ago. Two men came into the room, tied up Mr. Stauffer and forced Mrs. Stauffer at the point of a gun to go away with them. This man"—he pointed to Whitey—"was the one who freed Mr. Stauffer."

"Get off early?" I asked Whitey. "Race Cavanaugh's place doesn't close at ten o'clock."

"I just walked out," Whitey said. "Had a hunch."

"Good hunch," I said.

I looked at my watch. It said ten-thirty. I shook it. It was running all right. I couldn't believe that everything had happened in such a short time.

"We've sent out a call to have Mrs. Stauffer located," Masterson said. "I thought maybe you could help us."

"They been out of circulation for a while," Brown said.

"From what I've heard about the ease you're working on," Masterson said, "—and I must say I think you've caused the Chicago authorities plenty of headaches—it is possible that Lloyd Gantner is mixed up in Mrs. Stauffer's abduction."

"Doubtless," said Singer.

Masterson looked at Gorilla.

"You work for Gantner?" he asked.

The gorilla sneered.

"All I have to say is that I demand the right to call my lawyer."

A nasty look came over Peter Brown's face.

"Got no time for that nonsense," he said. "Where would they take Julia Stauffer?"

"I don't know."

Peter Brown kicked his shin. Gorilla squealed and grabbed his leg. Brown brought his big fist up against Gorilla's jaw and he straightened up.

"Where?" Brown said.

"I didn't have anything to do with—"

Brown hit him again.

"My lawyer will hear about this," Gorilla said.

Whitey walked over.

"Let me hit him," he said. "I ain't a cop."

Brown laughed.

"I'm not worried," he said.

Masterson said, "Wait a minute, Pete." He stepped up to Gorilla. "You've been Gantner's trouble shooter for ten years. You know everything about his business. If he had Mrs. Stauffer picked up, you'd know where he'd take her. We want to know that."

"Take it somewhere else," the guy said.

"I'm in a position—" Masterson started, and Gorilla said, "Nuts."

Suddenly Jerry came to life. He had been quiet as a mouse all the time. Now he turned on the Gorilla. He screamed at him.

"You lousy murderer! You didn't have no reason in the world to shoot these two guys"—pointing at Singer and me. "But you would've done it. You let Mac get knocked off because you wanted to shoot a cop. You got us in a fine mess. Now you got to be smart and clam up on the D.A. You dumb bastard. I'm through with you. I'm talkin'."

"Shut up!" said Gorilla savagely

"Go ahead," Masterson said to Jerry.

Gorilla took a step. Brown kicked him in the back of the legs and hit him in the neck. The gorilla fell on his face.

"All right," Masterson said to Jerry. "Let's have it."

"Honest," Jerry said, "I didn't have nothin' to do with shootin' these guys. I didn't even have a gun. I ain't got a gun now."

"All right," Masterson said tiredly. "Go ahead. What about Mrs. Stauffer?"

"If Gantner took her," Jerry said, "he probably took her to an apartment on Oak Street, near the Drake. He keeps the apartment, but he don't live in it. The number is 206. The apartment number is 41. He'd used it before when he had somebody picked up."

Masterson nodded at Brown.

"Let's go," he said. He looked at the other two cops. "You stay here with these crooks until headquarters gets a car here."

"Can I go?" Whitey asked.

Masterson looked annoyed.

"Sure, you can all go. You'll have to come, too, Mr. Batts, I guess, because somebody will have to identify Mrs. Stauffer."

Singer went to Frank and held out his hand.

"So do I, Singer," Frank said.

Masterson and Brown went out. Whitey and Singer and I followed. I closed the door on Frank Stauffer, the two mugs and the cops who were waiting for the wagon.

We went out the back way again and Masterson's car, a Cadillac, was parked next to Brown's. Singer, Whitey and I got in the back seat and Brown and Masterson in front. Masterson backed it onto the street, wheeled sharply to the right and got away with his tires squeaking.

Nobody said anything as we drove fast through the traffic on Michigan. Then we were waiting for a light.

"It will be in the first block," Brown said.

We turned into Oak Street and Masterson raced to the middle of the block, slowed suddenly, then stopped. His tires scraped the curb.

"Take it easy," Whitey said. "You can't get a car like this every day."

"This is it," Masterson said in his tired voice.

We all got out and walked up to the door of the apartment building. It was pretty fancy, dimly lighted, respectable, rich-looking. The lobby was all crystal and onyx.

Number 41 was on the fourth floor. We got in the elevator and Brown pushed the button. Nobody spoke as we rode up.

"You got a gun?" Brown asked me as we stepped into the fourth floor hall.

"Nope."

"Too bad," Brown said. "You'd better follow me."

We went down the corridor, looking at the numbers we passed and 41 was in the back corner. Brown went to the door and knocked, his gun small and stolid in his hand. I wished I had one. I was still shaky.

He knocked again and a voice said, "Who is it?"

"Police," Brown said.

The door opened. There was a guy who might have been a butler. He was putting on his coat and he had the right combination of courtesy and dead-pan in his face.

"Yes?" he said.

"Where's Gantner and the woman?" Brown asked.

"I beg your pardon?"

"Where are they?"

"I'm not sure I—"

"We'll come in."

Brown had put his gun away. He pushed past the butler and we all went inside.

It was an expensively furnished apartment, large and well kept. It didn't look as if anybody really lived in it, but it looked as if it would be ready to live in any time you wanted to.

The butler followed us through the vestibule into the living room.

"What is this all about?" he asked.

He was just asking the questions you would expect him to ask. He didn't seem to have any personal interest in it. "Is this Lloyd Gantner's apartment?" Masterson asked.

"Yes," the butler said, "though he doesn't use it now—only occasionally."

"He used it tonight, didn't he?"

"He was here tonight, yes."

"Alone?"

The guy looked around at all of us.

"Ah—you're from the police?"

Masterson took out a card. Brown flashed his badge.

"There was a woman with him. I hope there hasn't been any trouble. Has anything happened to Mr. Gantner?"

"Not yet—that I know of. Where did they go?"

"Look here—" the butler started.

Brown said, "None of that 'look here' stuff. Just answer the questions."

"I don't know where they went."

"Nuts!" Masterson said. "Brown, search the house. You help." He pointed at Whitey, who went off with Brown.

"When did they come to the apartment?" Masterson asked the butler.

"About an hour ago."

"Was the woman all right?"

"She seemed to be well. I couldn't quite understand why Mr. Gantner had—er—taken up with her—"

"That's neither here nor there. You say they went away. When did they leave?"

"A short time ago—less than twenty minutes, I would judge."

"Did they say where they were going?"

"Not to me."

"Did they say it to anybody?"

"There wasn't anybody else here."

Masterson's face kept looking more and more tired. "All right. Did they say anything out loud about where they were going?"

"It seems to me the woman kept saying, 'I can't tell you, Lloyd, I don't know,' and Mr. Gantner said, 'All right, then we'll go back there now and find it. You'll come, too.'"

Masterson looked at us.

"Preston?" I said.

The butler looked dumb.

"Were they going to catch a train?"

"I believe Mr. Gantner said something about there being a train at eleven-forty."

"That could be it," I said. "The eleven-forty to Wabash out of here goes through Preston Junction at 3:30 A.M."

"It must be that," Singer said. "I am amazed, but I can't doubt it."

Brown and Whitey came back.

"Nobody here," Brown said.

Singer was at the door.

"We can't delay any longer," he said. "It is of the utmost importance that Joseph and I return to Preston at once."

"We missed that eleven-forty," I said. "No other train for four hours."

"Then we'll have to find another way."

"We could make it in Frank Stauffer's car in three and a half hours, if you let me drive."

"Not only do I allow you," Singer said, "I implore you."

"Let's go," I said.

Masterson and Brown seemed confused, but I guess Singer had them convinced. They came with us fast and we all went down and piled into Masterson's car.

"Too bad you got to go so soon," Whitey said.

"Want to come along?" I asked.

"Can't. Got to work. I'm legitimate now."

He said it loud, hoping Masterson would hear it. Masterson didn't pay any attention.

Brown looked back at Singer.

"You got the case solved?" he asked.

"I wouldn't say so," Singer said. "But I know enough to realize that we must get back home before Julia and Gantner."

"Good luck," Brown said.

"I wish you would continue your check here tonight," Singer said, "in case the butler was trying to mislead us—"

"All right," Masterson said, and you could hear in his voice that he was fed up with the whole business.

We pulled up once more behind the hotel. Again we all got out and went up to the room. Singer went into our room and went to the telephone. I heard him ask the operator for the sheriff's office in Montpelier. I went into Frank's room.

The mugs and the two cops were gone. Frank was lying on the bed. He got up when I went in.

"We're going back to Preston, fast," I said. "We've got to use your car. Want to come along?"

"What did you find out?"

"Evidently Gantner took Julia back to Preston. They were trying to get the eleven-forty train."

Frank got his bag and started throwing things in it.

"My God," he said. "You can't tell what he might do."

"Singer's calling Sheriff Whitley," I said. "Will you call for your car? We haven't got much time."

"Certainly," Frank said.

I went back into our room.

Whitey and Brown were sitting on the sofa. Singer was still at the telephone. Masterson stood by the door.

"We'd better be on our way," he said to Brown.

I shook Brown's hand.

"Thanks, pal," I said. "You've got free room and board any time you come to Preston."

He grinned.

"Why would I come to Preston?" he said.

"God knows."

He went out with Masterson.

Whitey was eyeing the half-full bottle of whisky on the table.

"Help yourself," I said, throwing stuff into our bag. I took a twenty out of my pocket and handed it to him. "This room's engaged till tomorrow. Hang around and pay for it, will you? It won't be this much. Keep the change and finish that whisky."

"Okay," Whitey said. "Look, when you sleep in a bed like that—do you sleep on the mattress, or in between those white things?"

This was an old joke between us. There had been a time when neither of us knew, and Whitey found out before I did. It was a very corny joke, but in a way it made me homesick. I gave him the same old answer: "Any way it's comfortable, Whitey."

"Okay," he grinned.

Singer hung up the phone. He had a tight look on his face. I knew there was trouble.

"Sheriff Whitley isn't in and can't be reached," he said. "I consider it urgent that somebody be there when Julia and Gantner get in."

I looked at Whitey.

"Listen," I said. "You hang around here. Every fifteen minutes you call the sheriff's office in Montpelier. Keep trying till you get him. When you get him, tell him you're calling for Singer Batts, that Julia Stauffer and Lloyd Gantner are coming in on the three-thirty train and that Singer wants him to keep his eye on them. Got it?"

"I got it. This sheriff—he's all right?"

"He's fine. He'll do whatever you tell him, if you mention Singer."

I picked up the bag, thought of something.

"One more thing," I said to Whitey. "After you get through with the sheriff, I want you to put in another call, for me. To Miss Genevieve Sikes,

R-830. Tell her I'm moving too fast to call her myself, but I would like to have a date with her tomorrow night."

Singer's face was strained. Whitey looked at me as if I were crazy. I looked first at one of them, then the other. "Goddamn it," I said, "I feel like tomorrow night I'm going to be ready for a little female companionship. What's wrong with that?"

"Nothing," Whitey said. "Nothing, Joe. That's fine."

"Well, all right, then."

"Okay. Take it easy," Whitey said.

"Thanks, pal," I said. "Come and see us sometime."

"Sometime—maybe," Whitey said.

I carried our bag. Singer went ahead of me into Frank's room. Frank was packed and waiting.

"The car is ready," he said. "I had it filled up."

"Thanks," I said. "You mind if I drive?"

"I was hoping you would."

We went out, turned off the light and went downstairs. Frank went to the desk and paid for his room. The clerk looked at me. I told him about Whitey. We went out of the lobby and got into Frank's car. Frank got in back and Singer and I in front. I drove fast down Michigan to Monroe, over to the Outer Drive, to the South Side and got straightened out toward South Chicago and Hammond. The traffic was light and I had no trouble moving along.

After I got out of the thick of it, beyond Gary and headed for Michigan City, Singer switched on the strong dashlight and got the map out of his pocket. I glanced into the mirror. Frank was asleep in the back seat.

CHAPTER SIXTEEN

The road east of Gary is monotonous and I was already sleepy. I caught myself twice with my eyes closed and the car on the wrong side of the road. It made me nervous and I slowed down for a while. But I couldn't keep that pace. I had three hours of very fast driving to do if we were to beat Julia's train back to Preston. I had my window rolled down and I opened the ventilator as far as it would go.

There was little traffic. The road was narrow and white and cottages and farmhouses on both sides of the road sat dark and empty looking. Now and then a light would blink in one of them. When the headlights came from the opposite direction, it blinded me and I had to keep getting used to it all over again. But the car handled easily and made beautiful time. I decided to tell Frank Stauffer that I would buy it from him when he got ready to get another.

Singer was studying the map, patiently ignoring the occasional bumps and lurches.

"Talk to me," I said to him, "or I'll go to sleep."

Singer sighed deeply.

"Are you serious?" he asked.

"I'm serious as all hell."

"On what subject would you like to have me speak?"

I looked at him.

"There's more than one?"

He didn't say anything for a while. He sat looking out the window.

Then he looked around and said, "I've been wondering what Gantner told us—about that drive from the Junction around behind the Graves place."

"You think that's the way it was done?"

"It seems almost inevitable. Anyone driving into the Graves place, or out of it, at the hour of the murder, would have been noticed by someone."

"Maybe not."

"Maybe not. But probably. It might have been managed on foot."

"Why not?"

I was just talking to keep myself awake. I wasn't really following him. Now that I think it over, I guess he just talked to try to keep me awake.

"What about the double-cross angle?" I asked.

"As to the relationship between Candy and Gantner?"

"Yeah."

"I've thought of that."

"You don't think much of it?"

"Not much."

I looked at my watch. It was one-thirty and we had a hundred miles to go. I'd have to average fifty to make it. We'd been doing that all right, but I knew I couldn't keep it up safely without stimulation.

We were on the main truck route between Cleveland and Chicago. Up ahead was an all-night filling station, with a small cafe at one side. I slowed, turned in and stopped.

"Coffee," I said.

Frank Stauffer sat up.

"Trouble?" he asked.

"No. I need a cup of coffee. Want to come?"

"No," he yawned. "I'll go back to sleep."

We went into the cafe, sat down at the counter and ordered coffee and doughnuts. Singer wouldn't eat any doughnuts when they came.

"You haven't eaten anything since lunch yesterday," I said.

"I ate dinner."

"You just ate around the edges. Why don't you eat?"

"I don't enjoy eating. I'm never hungry. Must I eat?"

"Too much nervous energy."

Singer smiled.

"Perhaps," he said.

He looked at the clock on the wall.

"Will we be able to get there before that train?"

"Sure," I said. "Is it important?"

"It's more important than you have any idea."

"We'll make it."

We finished the coffee, went out and got back in the car. I tried to get Singer to talk, but he wouldn't, so I clamped my teeth together, got my head as near the window as possible and prayed that I'd stay awake.

Except for a few trucks the traffic had now died out completely. Since the road was as flat as a dance floor, the trucks weren't any problem. I got it up to seventy and managed to keep it there steadily enough to maintain my average. Frank's big car purred like a kitten.

Be fun if she threw a shoe, I thought, then quit thinking about it right away.

Twenty miles west of Preston we turned off the highway and got on the county road. I took a few big gulps of fresh air and hung on. I had begun to see two roads where there only should have been one. But I held it to a fairly straight line and we crossed the bridge and coasted up to the front entrance of the Hotel Preston without dents in the fenders, and exactly at three-fifteen.

Frank Stauffer woke up.

"Home?" he said. "You don't mind if I drive up to the Junction to meet Julia? I'm a little worried."

"By all means, go ahead," Singer said. "Joseph and I will use his car. Thank you for bringing us back."

"Joe did the bringing, I think," Frank said.

We climbed out and Frank got in the front seat. He waved as he turned the corner at Oak Street and straightened out to the north toward Preston Junction.

"I thought we were going to meet the train," I said. "I thought that was the whole idea."

"We were," Singer said, walking up the hotel steps. "But I caught sight of Sheriff Whitley in the lobby and assumed he had taken care of it. We don't have to meet the train. We have more urgent business."

Sheriff Whitley was sitting in a big chair in the lobby. Beside him, in another chair, was one of his deputies—the one I'd had the talk with out on the road after Gantner knocked me out.

The sheriff jumped up when we walked in and came over to meet us. He started right in—got right down to brass tacks.

"I got your message," he said. "There are two men at the Junction waiting for the train. They'll stick close to Gantner, but won't pick him up. Right?"

"That's right," Singer said. He turned to me. "Joseph, go get a shovel, a lantern and your gun. Make sure that both the gun and the lantern are filled."

I was too sleepy to be surprised. I went and got the stuff. When I got back to the lobby the sheriff was putting the map in his pocket. I could see by the grim look on his face that Singer had told him a lot. He looked well informed. "We'll take my car," Sheriff Whitley said.

We went outside again. The sheriff's car was parked out in front. I threw the stuff in the back seat with the deputy. Singer and I got in front with the sheriff.

The sheriff drove fast down Front Street. It was after three-thirty now. It seemed all out of joint to be speeding down that sleepy, dark little street with a shovel and a lantern and a gun, probably waking people up so that they would turn over in bed and mutter, "Damn kids, racin' around town."

My head was aching from the pounding I'd got and the strain of driving. When I closed my eyes I felt dizzy. But mostly I was confused. I had figured out only one possible place we might be going and this was the wrong direction. I looked at Singer. He was sitting very stiff and straight, looking ahead, not saying anything.

The sheriff stopped suddenly, apparently at some signal from Singer. We were in front of Jim Dennis' house. I started to look at Singer again, but gave it up.

Sheriff Whitley got out of the car and went up to Jim Dennis' door. I heard him knocking loudly. Probably a lot of people heard him. It was a still night and everybody was asleep and the knock sounded like somebody hitting a loose board with a sledge hammer.

He knocked several times and finally a light went on. We waited. I could see the outline of the sheriff standing on Jim's porch.

After a while the light went out and the sheriff and Jim Dennis came down the steps and over to the car. Jim climbed into the back seat and the sheriff got back under the wheel and we turned around and headed back toward the hotel.

"We didn't have time to stop in your house to talk to you, Jim," Singer said. "We had to ask you to come along."

"All right," Jim said, yawning. "What's the trouble?"

"I've got to ask you a few questions."

"Go ahead. Maybe I don't know the answers."

"Maybe not."

"Go ahead," Jim said again.

"You were out at the Graves place the night of the murder?"

"I've already admitted it."

Singer's voice was very quiet—but loud enough to carry, above the sound of the motor, to the back seat.

"I'm asking you," he said.

"Yeah, I was," Jim said. "What of it?"

"Don't ruffle your feathers, Jim. I haven't accused you of anything. I just need to know a few facts."

"I was there."

"Did you see anybody?"

"Yeah. I saw this woman that was staying there. I saw her but I didn't know who she was."

"You didn't see anybody else?"

There was a pause.

Finally Jim said, "Yeah. I saw somebody else'

"Inside the house, or outside?"

"Inside."

"Who was it?"

"I don't know. I couldn't see that well."

"You didn't go inside the house yourself?"

"No. After I saw I didn't know the woman I didn't care about getting inside."

There was a silence.

Then Singer said, "Jim—I don't like to say this, but you're lying. I know you went inside the house."

"You seem to know everything," Jim Dennis said.

"Not everything, Jim. Almost, but not quite."

"Well, what if I did go inside?"

"Well?" Singer said.

After another pause, Jim started talking.

"Here it is," he said. "I didn't kill the woman. I know it looks like I might have, but I didn't. That's why I've been holding out on you. I went out there in the first place because she sent for me. That was the first day she got here, about nine o'clock at night. My phone rang and this voice said it was Linda Graves, and would I come out. Something was wrong with one of the pipes in the kitchen.

"I went right out. As soon as I saw her, I knew she wasn't Linda Graves. There wasn't anything wrong with the pipes in the kitchen, either. She let me fuss around with them for a while, then she got down to business. She told me there was fifty thousand dollars buried in the back yard. I laughed at her, told her the people around town had quit believing that old story about Seth Graves burying some money a long time ago. She said she knew it was there and she said that if I would help her find it, she'd split it with me.

"I just laughed at her some more. I wasn't going to waste my time hunting around for a bunch of dough I didn't believe in. So I went away.

"Then I got to thinking it over, and I thought—maybe she's got something after all. I couldn't help thinking that a piece of fifty thousand dollars would help me out a lot. The reason I didn't turn her in as somebody living in the house who didn't belong there was that if she really had something, I wanted a piece of it.

"The night of the murder I decided to go back out there. I looked in the window—where Esmerelda Granger saw me—to make sure the coast was clear. Then I went to the front door and let myself in, with the key I've got.

"I told her I'd been thinking it over and maybe she was right, and if she still wanted me to help her, I would. I sat down on the bed in her bedroom there and she dug around in her purse and came up with this map. It was all wadded up in a little ball and I asked her about that and she said she usually kept it hidden on her. She didn't say where."

"That's why you wanted to examine the corpse in Jim Fisk's preparation room?"

"Yeah." Jim sounded a little sheepish. "She showed me the map and I figured out from it about where the money would be buried. She wouldn't tell me where she got the map.

"Funny thing—I just now remembered it—there was a little packet of letters on the dresser in her room. They were tied up with a piece of string. I noticed them and read what was on the top one. It was addressed to Linda Graves.

"Anyway, she had me pretty well convinced what with the map, with Seth Graves' name on it and all, and I told her I would help her find the money if she still wanted me to. I said I would have to go get some tools and that I'd be back."

I'd got so interested in Jim's story that I hadn't noticed where we'd gone. It was a shock to find out we were not moving any more. We were parked in the drive of the Graves place. There was no moon and the trees and bushes rose up black all around us.

Jim went on: "I left then and went out the back way, through the kitchen and back porch."

"You said you'd seen somebody in the house."

"Yeah. When I went out through the kitchen, I saw somebody over in one corner, somebody against the wall, away from the faint light coming in the window, standing still, just standing there."

Singer's quiet voice came out with the sixty-four-dollar question.

"Who was it?"

"It was too dark," Jim said. "I couldn't tell."

"Was it a man or a woman?"

There was a very long pause. I thought Jim hadn't heard the question and I kept waiting for Singer to repeat it. But he just waited and after a long time, Jim Dennis said, "It was a woman."

CHAPTER SEVENTEEN

The sheriff climbed out of the car and started giving orders.

"Hal," he said to his deputy, "light that lantern and bring it along. I'll go first. Joseph here can bring the shovel."

I was so tired I was batty.

"Oh, goody," I said. "We're going to hunt for buried treasure."

Singer turned his head sharply and looked at me. It almost knocked the wind out of me. It wasn't like Singer. His face was hurt and angry.

"Sorry," I mumbled. "I didn't mean to be flippant." He put his hand on my shoulder. That was rare for Singer, too. I suddenly remembered what Jim Dennis had said. "It was a woman."

I looked at Singer and felt a little sick. He shook his head and smiled a little.

"No, Joseph," he said quietly. "It's not what you think." The sheriff and Hal and Jim Dennis had gone on up the drive toward the Graves house. Singer and I followed, me carrying the shovel.

It was very dark. No light at all came through the trees and shrubbery and we had to stay close to the lantern to keep from stumbling. A low wind had come up and it moaned and sighed through the high branches of the trees. When we got close enough to see the house it stuck up, gray and like a box, looking ugly and worn out and dead.

The sheriff led the way around the corner of the front porch and back along the south wall of the house toward the barn. At the corner of the barn nearest the house he stopped and looked around at Singer, who nodded.

"Set the lantern down here, Hal," the sheriff said.

"Jim," Singer said, "I think you remember where Linda buried her dog, Barcus."

Jim looked startled.

"Why the hell should I—?" he sighed, said, "Yeah. I helped her."

"Would you point it out to us?"

"I'll try," Jim said.

The sheriff hauled out a big flashlight and Jim struck off into the tangled mass of brambles and deep grass that made up the back lot of the Graves place. Jim went first, carrying the flashlight. The sheriff followed him and Singer and I came along after that. About in the center of the lot, Jim stopped. He looked around, his face puzzled.

"There's a marker," he said.

There was a small gravestone, sticking up at an angle. It was old, worn and encrusted with moss and dirt. You couldn't read anything on it.

"But that's not where the dog was buried," Jim said.

"Yes," Singer said. "I know."

Jim hesitated a moment, then went on toward the back. There were some dense bushes and we had to push through them, ducking when the branches snapped back at our faces.

Jim stopped beside a small fruit tree. He searched the ground carefully, walked a few feet to the north, then stood, pointing downward.

"This ought to be it," he said. "It's as close as I can come."

The sheriff looked toward the corner of the barn.

"Hold the lantern up, Hal!" he called.

In a moment, we saw the reddish glow of the lantern. Singer faced it and began pacing his way toward it... Seven...eight...nine...ten. Singer stopped. Once more the sheriff called to his deputy.

"Bring it over here, Hal."

Hal came stumbling through the brush, carrying the lantern. The sheriff set it on the ground near where Singer stood.

"Turn it down as far as you can," he said, "and still leave Joseph some light."

"Me?" I croaked.

I was scared. The whole thing suddenly seemed like a nightmare.

The sheriff pointed at the ground.

"Right here," he said. "Dig."

"I know you're tired," Singer said. "We'll take turns."

"Oh, I can dig," I said. "I'm just a little confused."

I jabbed the shovel into the earth. It was soft and there were no roots. It wouldn't be hard work.

Jim Dennis stood around, watching me. Suddenly he stepped up and grabbed the shovel.

"Christ's sake," he said. "Let me do it."

I was glad to let him. He plowed in at a great rate. I moved back a step to keep some of the dirt out of my eyes. Singer stood silent, watching. His face in the glow of the lantern looked grim and unhappy.

I took the shovel again to give Jim Dennis a rest. He had got down four or five feet now in a hole about three feet across. It was easy going.

Jim moved off a little way, out of the ring of light thrown by the lantern. His voice came suddenly out of the darkness.

"That map was nuts," he said.

"Yes?" said Singer, very quietly.

"It couldn't even have been made."

"No?" Singer whispered.

"Hell, no. It was dated 1925. Seth Graves was blind as a bat in 1925."

For sonic reason that made me sore. Everything looked futile and silly. I jammed the shovel down into the hole as hard as I could. It struck something hard. It might have been a rock, but it was smooth because the shovel slipped off it and whatever it was rolled away.

Bring the lantern, I thought I said, but then realized that I had only thought it. I tried again.

"Bring the lantern."

The sheriff brought it over and set it down at the edge of the hole. I bent down and pushed into the dirt with my fingers. They grabbed onto something hard and I pulled on it. Singer and Jim Dennis were bending over the hole, peering down.

What I pulled up was round and smooth, like the handle of the shovel. I held it up to the light.

"Jesus Christopher!" said Jim Dennis. "It's a piece of skeleton."

"Fine," I said. "But whose?"

Singer's voice, suddenly tired, came from a long way off.

"It's the buried treasure," he said. "You'll find the rest of it, if you'll look long enough." He paused. "It's the skeleton of Linda Graves."

For about five seconds there was a hush as solid, as black, as deep as Linda's grave. Then, off in the trees somewhere somebody yelled, "Look out!" and without thinking at all I ducked down into the hole.

There was a sharp crack and a splinter of glass and the light went out. I heard feet smashing through the brush and a lot of thrashing around. There was another sharp crack and a little scream, then nothing.

I climbed out of the hole. Somebody with a flashlight was hurrying toward a clump of trees about thirty feet away. I followed, not hurrying.

When I got there it was quite a little group. There were the sheriff, his deputy Hal, Jim Dennis and Singer and a couple of the sheriff's other deputies. Also, there were Lloyd Gantner, Frank Stauffer and Julia Stauffer. Julia was lying on the ground in a big heap, and everybody was standing around looking down at her. I tried to look down at her but felt sick to my stomach.

I got a bellyful of death, I thought.

"She had the gun out before I realized it," Gantner was saying. "I reached for it, but it was too late."

"I fired at the sound," Sheriff Whitley said. He looked at Frank Stauffer. "I'm sorry."

"Never mind," said Frank softly. "Someday it had to happen."

I held onto my stomach and looked down at the body of Julia Stauffer.

"She did it?" I asked.

"She killed Linda Graves," Singer said, trying to look at Frank, but not having much success.

"She didn't kill Candy, too?" I said.

There was a pause.

Then Frank Stauffer said, "No, Joe. I did."

Lloyd Gantner's face took on a strange twisted look. He stooped suddenly, swept up the gun that lay beside Julia's body and aimed it at Frank Stauffer. Sheriff Whitley, without seeming to move, brought his gun barrel down on Gantner's wrist so hard you could hear it crack. He dropped the gun and grabbed his wrist.

Singer's voice was hard.

"You are a bad loser," he said to Gantner. "It was your own doing. You and your paramour were blackmailing Mr. Stauffer. It became insupportable. He had to kill the woman to stop it."

"I don't know what you're talking about," Gantner said.

"I think you do," Singer said. "Frank—am I right?"

"You're right, Singer. How long have you known?"

"I began to guess at it the day after the murder," Singer said, "when you showed us the letters. It was always the letters. There was something too good about them, too pat. Blackmail was an inevitable conclusion. The stranger's presence in town had to be connected with the letters. Also, at the time you showed us the letters, when I asked you what you thought about the case you said there had to be some reason for a woman to come down here *from Chicago*. Nothing had been established about her being from Chicago. I knew you knew something about the woman that you hadn't admitted.

"When I guessed that you were being blackmailed, I had to assume that something was wrong about the Graves estate. The long search, the trip to Chicago, all the seemingly irrelevant chasing about was an attempt to find out what had happened to Linda Graves and when. I didn't dare tell anyone what I was doing—even Joseph. I didn't dare take a chance on your being able to cover up."

Frank was looking down at his dead wife.

"She killed Linda after we were married," he said. "She got drunk and lost her head. She trapped me into marrying her with a story about being pregnant. I confess, it might have been. But afterward I found it wasn't true.

"Julia had an obsession that Linda was just waiting for me to get rid of her and then I would return to Linda. She got drunk and wild and came out here. I followed her, but I was too late. Linda and Julia were in the garden. Julia had a gun. She was a good shot. Linda saw me coming and called to me. Julia ran off, turned and shot at Linda. It killed her instantly. Julia ran away.

"It was late afternoon and I carried Linda into the pergola and sat there, waiting till dark. Seth was away at the time; Si, the caretaker, was on his vacation. There was nobody.

"After dark I dug a grave and buried Linda. I knew Seth wouldn't be back for a week or ten days. I worked the ground over the grave carefully and replaced the ferns and flowers that had been growing there. By the time Seth returned there was nothing to notice.

"I went in the house and wrote a farewell note to Seth from Linda. I didn't know how I got away with it. I wrote it on Linda's typewriter and forged her signature. I did the same with the letters to me I showed you. It was only a step from there to the Candy woman.

"I met her in Chicago a few days after Linda's death. Gantner wasn't around then. Somebody I knew introduced me to Candy and I offered her a hundred dollars a week for writing letters to Seth and me—from Linda. She could do anything she wanted to do, go anywhere. I would send her copies of the letters I wanted written and she would write them and post them from wherever she happened to be. I told her it was because Linda had run away and her father had lost his reason and as long as he got letters from her it would help keep him more or less steady. I had her write to me, too, in order to keep Seth convinced.

"It couldn't work forever. About ten years ago she started to shake me down. That was after she'd taken up with Gantner. She raised her price.

"It was too late for me to stop. I had paid her out of the Graves estate, making the checks out to Linda Graves. Just as I told you last week—the money ran out. I had none of my own left."

Sheriff Whitley shook his head.

"You must have gone through a lot of hell."

"Yes," Frank said. "Why I did it, I don't know. I had some feeling I had to protect Julia. I don't know—"

"The map?" I asked.

"The map was a mistake. Gantner and Candy guessed that I was about out of money and I had to keep them contented. I told them Seth buried fifty thousand dollars and tried to make a deal with them to call the whole thing off."

"You never can," the sheriff said, looking at Gantner.

"No," Frank said. "You never can."

"What happened when this girl came to town the other day?"

"I think Singer knows," Frank said.

"When Candy came to town," Singer said, "I think she called Frank and he came out to see her. She told him she knew he had killed Linda Graves and she wanted money. When Frank said he didn't have it, she said he'd have to get it, that she would stay here in the Graves house till he did.

She couldn't have stayed long without bringing everything to light after the town's curiosity had risen to the boiling point.

"Frank went out there the night of the murder, intending to persuade her to leave town. He offered her some money—nothing like fifty thousand dollars—and I think he also offered to throw in his wife's mink coat, which he had with him."

Jim Dennis broke in.

"That's why I thought I saw a woman in the kitchen. He had that coat with him and he put it over him when he heard me coming."

"I think so," Singer said. "Candy spurned Frank's offer. She had guessed that the map actually showed the location of Linda's grave and she told Frank she would dig it up and confront the law with it if he didn't give her what she asked.

"It was a hopeless situation for Frank. The letters he'd written to Candy, addressed to Linda Graves, were lying on the dresser, taunting him. He was hemmed in. He grabbed the letters and there was a struggle over them. Frank got them, but a corner got torn off, the corner we found. He was aroused by this time and he had only one alternative anyway. He strangled her. He probably used his leather watch chain. It would leave a faint blue mark, such as we found on the woman's throat."

Singer paused.

"You're right, almost exactly," Frank said. "I guess Gantner tried to pick up where Candy had stopped. His main object was to find the map. He sent his men down to get the body, because he knew she would hide the map somewhere on her person."

"It all seems very complicated," I said.

"It was too complicated," Frank said. "Julia sealed her doom when she took the map from the safe and gave it to Candy. I think Julia actually thought Candy and Gantner were convinced that it was money buried here."

He paused, looked at Singer for a long time and said, "I've had no hope of escape for the last three days. When Singer told me he had the map, I knew it was finished. Singer has that kind of imagination." He looked around the group. "It doesn't matter now. I'm an old man. I died twenty-five years ago, with Linda Graves."

Sheriff Whitley put his hand on Frank's arm. One of the deputies escorted Gantner. They walked away toward the big, gray, dead house and disappeared.

"My God," Jim Dennis said, "I need a drink."

One deputy had stayed with the body of Julia Stauffer. We said good night.

"Me, too," I said. "Let's go back to the hotel."

CHAPTER EIGHTEEN

Genevieve Sikes and I came out of the show and crossed the street. We walked around behind the hotel where the car was parked and climbed in. We drove slowly down Front Street, over the bridge and out along the dark county road.

"That was a good show," Genevieve said.

"It was a mystery," I said. "I hate mysteries."

Genevieve snuggled up close and patted my stiff cheeks.

"You'll get over it," she said.

"Let's turn up this little dark lane right here and get over it right now," I said.

She didn't say anything, so I turned up the little lane and we bumped along a few feet until the road was out of sight. There was a creek not far off, and the water gurgled softly.

Genevieve laid her head in the crook of my arm, and we just sat there for a while. She pulled my head down close and whispered to me, "Joe— don't look now, but—we're not alone."

"The hell we aren't."

"We aren't."

There was a sound in the back seat. Automatically my hand jumped to my coat pocket. I looked around slowly.

Climbing up from the floor to the back seat was my ever-loving Singer Batts. He got on the seat and looked at me foolishly.

I just looked. I couldn't say anything.

"Well—" Singer said at last, "you've been telling me I couldn't get a bride by correspondence. I thought—"

"Yeah?" I said, as his voice dwindled away.

"I thought I would just come along for a first-hand lesson in wooing."

I looked down at Genevieve. She was laughing.

"Don't make him walk back to town, darling," she said.

I kissed her.

www.ingramcontent.com/pod-product-compliance
Lightning Source LLC
Chambersburg PA
CBHW011448170626
46816CB00008B/2579